*Acting Edition*

# What Did We Do Wrong?

by Henry Denker

SAMUEL FRENCH

WHAT DID WE DO WRONG?, by Henry Denker, directed by Sherwood Arthur, was presented by Michael Myerberg and Donald Flamm at the Helen Hayes Theatre, New York.

## CHARACTERS
### (*In Order of Their Appearance*)

| | |
|---|---|
| NORMA DAVIS | *Philippa Bevans* |
| WALTER DAVIS, SENIOR | *Paul Ford* |
| WALTER DAVIS, JUNIOR | *Russell Horton* |
| SCOTT | *Gregory Rozakis* |
| CINDY | *Heidi Vaughn* |
| WOODY JACKSON | *Roy Providence* |
| CLARENCE CAHILL | *Hugh Franklin* |
| CHARLOTTE CAHILL | *Enid Markey* |

## SYNOPSIS OF SCENES

The living room of the Davis' meticulously decorated home in White Plains, New York.

## ACT ONE

SCENE 1: A spring evening.
SCENE 2: Early the next morning.

## ACT TWO

SCENE 1: Several hours later.
SCENE 2: Later that afternoon.

# What Did We Do Wrong?

## ACT ONE

### Scene 1

The Time: *An evening in spring.*

The Place: *The Davis home in White Plains. The action takes place in the living room. Upstage is a wide archway with stairway to upper floor. It is a conventional home, better-than-average middle class. It is comfortable, traditional, warm, and well-decorated. At R. is the door to sun parlor, garage, etc.*

At Rise: Norma Davis, *the lady of the house, is curled up on a comfortable sofa, L. A dial phone is on end table at Upstage end of sofa, L. Norma is a trim suburban housewife, a "doer," attractive, well-conditioned. She reads. Mostly uplift and "serious" books. Also, McCalls, Parents Magazine, and, as she is doing right now, The Reader's Digest. On Stage, at rise, stands a roof-type TV antenna, preset L. of easy chair R.; large, fairly complex, tubes, rods, etc. Walter Davis enters from the kitchen-basement area U. R., carrying a weathervane in stainless steel, which he fits atop the antenna and spins.*

Norma. (*Suddenly.*) Did you know you can replace a whole human arm?

Walter. Who? Me?

Norma. The Doctors. The Doctors.

Walter. (*Relieved, uninvolved. He goes on working on the antenna.*) Is that so?

5

NORMA. (*Suddenly, more surprised.*) Good God!

WALTER. (*Concerned now.*) Norma! What happened?

NORMA. There's one doctor working on transplanting a whole human brain! (*He shakes his head; that's Norma for you.*) That way when the body of some famous man wears out we could have the benefit of his brain practically forever. Isn't that marvelous?

WALTER. I guess so. (*To himself as he returns to work.*) If the Reader's Digest would only apply itself to some problem less than earth-shaking. But no! They "run" China. Teach do-it-yourself surgery. And find God. In every issue. (*More voice.*) How many times do you have to find God?

NORMA. What did you say?

WALTER. Why is He always getting lost? Why doesn't He get found and stay found?

NORMA. Who?

WALTER. God!

NORMA. Walter—please—don't be sacrilegious.

WALTER. You're right, Norma. I'm sorry. (*Taking an oath.*) I will never again criticize the Reader's Digest.

NORMA. (*Puts Reader's Digest on coffee table.*) Walter, what's wrong with you tonight?

WALTER. (*Crosses to her.*) Norma, our sales have been dropping.

NORMA. (*Casually.*) Have they?

WALTER. (*Sits in chair U. L.*) And some of our stockholders say it's the fault of our design.

NORMA. Well, you're the president not the designer. Let Harry worry about the design.

WALTER. I can't sit there in the stockholders' meeting and say sales would improve if our design would improve. After all, Harry is not only my brilliant treasurer and designer. He is also my brother-in-law.

NORMA. (*Rises.*) Harry is my brother is what you mean.

WALTER. (*Rises and crosses R.*) What a coincidence. Here! *My* new model. Designed especially for color TV.

NORMA. (*Follows him one step* R.) Walter, this is your home. Not the office or the lab.

WALTER. I don't want anyone in the office to see this till I present it at the stockholders' meeting next week.

NORMA. I don't want that clutter in the living room.

WALTER. Ever since you redecorated, it's like the Metropolitan Museum around here. Every day I expect to come home and find a uniformed guard.

NORMA. The years when Wally's friends used this place as a hamburger stand and discotheque are over!

WALTER. So are the years when a man could just come home and relax. Norma, does the whole burden of the cultural explosion have to fall on our shoulders? Couldn't someone else help a little?

NORMA. We're only catching up on the things we missed when I was busy with car pools and orthodontists. (*Crosses to him.*) You *should* look on this as a new freedom. A second honeymoon.

WALTER. I always *dreamed* of spending my second honeymoon at Lincoln Center.

NORMA. (*Turns away* L.) Don't start *that* again.

WALTER. How many times do we have to go *this* week?

NORMA. (*Returns to him, trying to minimize it.*) Only the opera and the play. (*Then remembering.*) Oh—and the Foreign Film Festival.

WALTER. (*Dismally.*) Great.

NORMA. (*Turns away.*) Other husbands seem to enjoy it!

WALTER. Norma, the average American business man—

NORMA. (*Interrupting.*) You didn't build WEATHER-VANE into a big company by being "average."

WALTER. (*Crosses Downstage around to* R. *of easy chair.*) No, I built it by going to foreign film festivals. (*Then, referring to antenna.*) Now what do you think of this new model?

NORMA. (*Crosses to antenna, studying it.*) It looks fine, just fine. (*She can never leave anything exactly as she finds it. She reaches for red bar on antenna.*) Of course, it might be better *this* way.

WALTER. Norma, don't touch *that* one! Sweetheart, that's the one that receives the signal.

NORMA. You mean all these others are not necessary?

WALTER. They *sell*. This one *receives*. And, of course, our trademark—stainless as ever.

NORMA. Yes, dear, "Weathervane is Stainless," and I love it, but it's eight o'clock.

WALTER. (*He knows what that means.*) Of course. Tuesday. Another "hilarious," "heart-warming" episode of "That's Our Dad"!

NORMA. (*Always self-conscious about liking it.*) So it's a silly show. I'm commenting on it in my speech. I *have* to watch it.

WALTER. Every week?

NORMA. (*Admitting, aggressively.*) I also happen to think it's funny. Besides, it's the only show I watch anymore.

WALTER. Then watch it in the sun parlor. (NORMA *starts* U. R.) That's the real trouble. Nobody wants to watch TV anymore. So what do they need antennas for?

NORMA. (*She interrupts her cross to sun parlor.*) So it *isn't* Harry's fault.

WALTER. What?

NORMA. Fourteen times in the last three days you have made nasty remarks about my brother Harry.

WALTER. I? Made nasty remarks about my dear designer, treasurer and brother-in-law? Why would I do that? Merely because he's ruined me, that's why!

NORMA. He was only a junior partner. He couldn't make you do anything. (*Beat, then softer.*) Stockholder trouble again? (*She crosses and kisses him consolingly.*) Clarence Cahill?

WALTER. Yeah. Clarence Cahill.

NORMA. I'm sorry.

WALTER. Some days I say to myself, let him take over!

Let *him* have the headaches of running the company. And *I'll* sit back and criticize.

NORMA. Well, why don't you? *Next* time they offer you the nomination for mayor, take it!

WALTER. They did. And I did.

NORMA. (*It was a delightful surprise.*) Walter!

WALTER. They had a luncheon for me at the City Club, yesterday.

NORMA. You never told me.

WALTER. You were at a committee meeting. So I told the cleaning woman. But I'm not going to give up Weathervane! If Cahill thinks I'm going to be sidetracked by a political office he's got another think coming. *I* built that company! From a one-room loft to a big air-conditioned plant. He just happens to own some stock. And he wouldn't even own that if your brother hadn't kept insisting, go public, go public.

NORMA. (*Crosses to sofa and sits.*) You must admit you did very nicely when you went public. Now you have money *and* a business.

WALTER. (*Moves to* C.) And headaches! Go public! Norma, this country was built by men who dreamed of being their own boss. Finally *I* became my own boss. Till you made me take Harry into the business. And he kept saying, go public, go public. Now, I have four hundred and six bosses. And damn near all of them live in this town. I go down to get a haircut and the barber asks me, how's business and I've got to tell him. Cause he's a stockholder.

NORMA. (*Rises.*) Well, I'm sure Harry only meant the best.

WALTER. Go public! If I had a chance to make one last plea to the businessmen of America I'd cry out, "Pass the word. Go private!"

NORMA. (*Exiting to the sun parlor.*) You always did have a tendency to over-dramatizing everything.

WALTER. (*Calling after her.*) If Cahill gets enough dissident stockholders to take control, next week—or the

Union goes out on strike as they've been threatening, you won't say I'm over-dramatizing! (*The PHONE rings; he answers it.*) Hello? . . . Long Distance? . . . Yes, yes, this is Walter Davis . . . Yes, right, Weathervane . . . What? . . . Oh, no. We're not exactly in TV. Though we do make antennas . . . That's right. So I'm afraid you have the wrong company. Better look it up in the Yellow Pages. (*Almost hangs up, then.*) Or the Reader's Digest! (*Hangs up phone, turns to antenna.*) Now, if we could just give *this* more sales appeal . . . (*He starts to re-arrange the bars but is interrupted by* NORMA's *Off-stage laugh at TV.* WALTER *with years of irritation over that show in his background, reacts to her laugh.*) And what is good old loveable stupid "Dad" doing *this* week?

NORMA. (*Off.*) Locked himself in the garage. (*She laughs again.*)

WALTER. And now?

NORMA. (*Off.*) He tried to get out the window. And his pants caught. So he's straddling the sill. Can't get out, can't get back in.

WALTER. And his seven-year-old son will have to show him how. Every week good old Jim gets stupider and stupider, if you believe *them*. (NORMA *laughs again.*) Some day, some day, every man in America is going to rise up— (*PHONE rings.*) and answer the telephone. (*Crosses to desk and phone.*) Hello! . . . Yes! Look, Long Distance, that man has the wrong Davis. *We* are not in television, but we make . . . *Sing? Me?* I'm lucky if they just let me talk these days . . . Say, wait a minute! Could you possibly want Walter Davis, *Junior?* . . . I thought so. He's my son. But he's away at school way up in New Hampshire. You can reach him at his fraternity house. That's Hathaway 7 . . . What? . . . No, we don't even *get* Channel 41 down here. Why? . . . Wally on TV? No kidding! Norma, Wally was on— (*He is interrupted by voice.*) Surprised? Why should I be surprised? That boy is a born leader. Always has been. Mind you, I'm not saying that because he's my son . . .

*What? What did you say?* . . . Now, see here, that's my *son* you're talking about! (NORMA, *unaware, laughs.*) Norma, stop laughing. It isn't funny!! (*Into phone again.*) You're sure it was Walter Davis, Junior? Of White Plains, New York? . . . I don't believe it! . . . Ask him? How can I ask him, he's not here. On his way . . . How do *you* know? Say, who are you anyway? . . . A reporter? Well, listen, what's this all about? . . . Hello! Hello! (*Stunned, he hangs up.*)

NORMA. (*Enters* U. R.) Now what were you getting so nasty about? Another call from a stockholder?

WALTER. This is about Wally!

NORMA. Wally? *Wally?* What *about* Wally?

WALTER. I just had a phone call.

NORMA. What about Wally? What happened?

WALTER. (*Crosses* R., *Upstage of her to* C.) Now, now, Norma—

NORMA. Walter Davis, you better tell me! Everything!

WALTER. I don't know everything.

NORMA. (*After him.*) *What happened to my baby?*

(BOTH *are at* C.)

WALTER. Norma, sweetheart, your "baby" was put in jail.

NORMA. Wally—my Wal—oh, *no!* (*She breaks.*)

WALTER. Now, now, he's out as I understand it. And they think he's on his way home. That was a reporter calling to interview him.

NORMA. Good God, what did he do?

WALTER. I didn't get that part.

NORMA. (*Suddenly.*) LSD!

WALTER. He didn't say anything about LSD.

NORMA. (*On her own tack.*) I read about it in McCall's. Those college boys and girls. That's all they do. Sit around and "turn on" and "take off" and "go go."

WALTER. Now, Norma, don't jump to conclusions. It's probably some harmless college-boy prank.

NORMA. (*On her own cloud.*) Well, if he did get arrested, I just hope he didn't *say* anything. Till he got a lawyer. The Digest had this article on that new Supreme Court decision on confessions—

WALTER. (*Trying to kid her out of it.*) I think that's only to protect confirmed criminals. Or is it Catholics? No, criminals can't confess in police stations. And Catholics can't confess in public schools. I don't think it applies to college students.

NORMA. This isn't anything to joke about, Walter!

WALTER. That boy didn't do anything really wrong. So don't quote me McCall's. Or the Reader's Digest.

NORMA. *You* could read more, you know. And I don't mean the sports pages and the market reports.

WALTER. Maybe I would, if they had an article titled, "How to Help Your Son Beat the Rap."

NORMA. (*Crosses* L. *to behind chair; suddenly.*) Call the college! I insist on talking to the Dean!

WALTER. Norma, sweetheart, please—

NORMA. If you don't, I will!

WALTER. (*As he crosses to phone.*) Why you have to make a Federal case out of a harmless little prank . . . (*He dials 211.* NORMA *crosses* R. *to library area.*) Operator, I would like to place a call to Dean—

NORMA. Stallings!

WALTER. (*Resents her supplying the name.*) Dean Stallings. Hathaway College. In New Hampshire . . . No, I'll hold on.

NORMA. (*Her mind spinning in its own orbit.*) I can't understand it. Oh, Walter, what did we do wrong? (*He shrugs wearily, that's* NORMA *for you.*) We did everything we were supposed to. (*She moves to bookshelf to lift out book.*) I followed this religiously! (*Crosses* C. *carrying Dr. Spock book.*)

WALTER. What's that, the Bible?

NORMA. (*Crossing to him.*) Doctor Spock!

WALTER. Well, look up and see what Spock says about bail.

NORMA. (*Crosses to sofa, sits.*) He's seen us through every crisis!

WALTER. Which we probably wouldn't have *had,* if we didn't follow that damn book. (WALTER *sits on chair* L. *while holding phone.*)

NORMA. (*Putting book on coffee table; a discovery.*) *I* know!

WALTER. What?

NORMA. *You! You* did it!

WALTER. (*Innocent, and confused.*) I did what?

NORMA. That time you hid his baseball glove for a whole week! There's nothing more *traumatic* for a child than deprivation!

WALTER. He wasn't deprivated! I mean, deprived. I took away his mitt till he mowed the lawn. Now, what's so traumatic about that? (*Sarcastically.*) If you ask me, I think it was *you.*

NORMA. (*Perfection indignant.*) *Me?* What did I do?

WALTER. You never should have weaned him.

NORMA. That's not very funny.

WALTER. It isn't? Think about it for a while.

NORMA. (*Conceding a bit.*) It—it could have been the toilet training.

WALTER. We had to do *something.*

NORMA. (*In her own orbit.*) He was never the same after that.

WALTER. Thank God!

NORMA. You know what I mean.

WALTER. I know what *I* mean.

NORMA. Walter, dear, there are several things that are out of date. Hoop skirts. Writing on stone tablets. And *your* ideas on how to bring up children.

WALTER. Well, my mother always used to—

NORMA. (*Dismissing her.*) Your mother . . .

WALTER. (*With exquisite sweetness.*) Norma, honey, sweetheart, why is it that in the whole twenty-two years of our marriage you have never once let me finish a sentence that begins with "My mother"?

NORMA. Right now I am not interested in "your mother."

WALTER. (*Almost to himself.*) I figured as much.

NORMA. *I* want to know what *we* did *wrong*.

WALTER. How can we tell what *we* did wrong till we know what *he* did wrong?

NORMA. That's the kind of logic that seems so reasonable but is completely fallacious!

WALTER. (*He hasn't won one yet.*) Naturally. (*Into phone to vent his burn.*) Damn it, operator, where the hell is that dean? . . . Oh, I'm sorry, very very sorry . . . Yes, yes, I know about profanity on the telephone . . . You'll do *what?* "Take out my instrument"? (*He looks into phone, then at* NORMA.) And *they* talk about profanity. (*Into phone.*) Oh, I see. He's not there . . . Well, did they say where he could be reached? . . . Thank you anyhow. (*Hangs up.*) He's not there. Probably down at the jail. Bailing out students. (WALTER *rises and puts phone back on table* L.)

NORMA. (*Rises and crosses* R. *to* C.) It's *your* fault.

WALTER. (*Crossing* R. *to* L. C.) The dean is out. How is that my fault?

NORMA. Wally! Your aggressive attitude. How can you *expect* your son to grow up right if *you* can't even get along with a telephone operator?

WALTER. Now that's the kind of logic that sounds fallacious. So it must be completely reasonable!

NORMA. (*She glares at him, then moves to him.*) When he gets home we can't appear to be angry! We have to be calm!

WALTER. Like you.

NORMA. (*She resents that but goes on.*) We have to face this intelligently and realistically! We have to listen to him first. Remember that time he was sent home from school for taking down that little girl's pants and you shouted at him?

WALTER. Yes, dear, I remember. Probably scarred him for life.

NORMA. Probably? Well, I can tell you that Doctor Spock said—

WALTER. *You* should have heard what the little girl's father said.

NORMA. (*Turns away.*) There you go again!

WALTER. Okay! Take out my instrument! (*But a worm in his own imagination begins to stir.*) You know, Norma, come to think of it—could he possibly have—? No, no, not Wally.

NORMA. What did you just think? Not—? (*She dreads suggesting but it is obvious* BOTH *of them have wicked suspicions.*)

WALTER. I'll tell, if you will.

NORMA. You first.

WALTER. Okay. He was caught fooling around with another student.

(BOTH *are at* C.)

NORMA. (*Dogmatically loyal.*) *Not Wally!*

WALTER. I meant a *girl* student.

NORMA. (*Assuaged somewhat.*) Maybe it *is* only sex. (*Convincing herself.*) Sex is not necessarily wrong. Especially if she's a nice girl. And not pregnant.

WALTER. Now, what did *you* think?

NORMA. Marijuana.

WALTER. He doesn't even smoke.

NORMA. Of course, Parents Magazine says marijuana is *not* addictive. On the other hand, it leads to experimentation. Which could mean—psychedelics! LSD!

WALTER. You mean, going on a cruise.

NORMA. Trip! Trip!

WALTER. Okay, trip! Now, Norma, he's a fine boy. A nice clean-cut young man any parents would be proud of. You've even used him as an example in some of your damn speeches—I mean brilliant lectures. At your Women's Club. So let's not accuse him of every crime in the book! (NORMA *crosses* D. L. *to coffee table and cries.*

WALTER *follows and comforts her.*) Norma, sweetheart, please. Whatever he did, we'll face it intelligently and realistically. Only don't cry. Please? (*She only cries the louder.* WALTER *turns away* R.) Your family are the biggest god-damndest criers!

NORMA. I'm sorry—but I started thinking, it doesn't matter *what* he did. He's my baby. And I'm going to stand by him.

WALTER. (*He crosses back to her.*) Exactly. That's all I've been trying to say. Now, make a little room for me.

(WALTER *edges close to her. She smiles and they kiss. And* BOTH *feel better for the moment, till she suddenly jumps up.*)

NORMA. (*Crosses* R.) Good God!

WALTER. (*Jumping up to face the next emergency.*) What? Norma, what happened?

NORMA. The supermarket closes at nine! If he *is* coming home, you'd better go down and get some milk! (*As he starts* U. L.) Six quarts!

WALTER. (*Halts.*) He went to jail. He didn't take poison.

NORMA. You *know* how he gulps milk when he's under nervous tension.

(WALTER *removes smock as he crosses up to coat rack on landing,* L. *Returns wearing cap and putting on jacket.*)

WALTER. Yes, mam. Maybe weaning him was a mistake.

NORMA. Walter, just go to the market.

WALTER. Yes, mam. (*Starts Upstage.*)

NORMA. (*Follows.*) Walter—

WALTER. (*Stops.*) Yes, mam.

NORMA. Stop saying "yes, mam" as if I were your mother. That's not a healthy relationship.

WALTER. Oh, for the old days. When it was all right
to be friends. Or husband and wife. Or lovers, even.
Today, everything is a relationship. And it's either healthy
or unhealthy. My mother used to—

NORMA. (*Interrupting.*) Walter, the market will be
closed.

WALTER. Yes, mam. (*Looks skyward.*) I keep trying,
Mother. (*He exits.*)

(NORMA *heads at once for the copy of Spock, starts hunt-
ing through it, using the back index and referring
to the text. But almost immediately the PHONE
rings. She answers it.*)

NORMA. Hello? . . . No, no, Walter isn't here . . .
Oh, Harry! Harry, the most terrible thing has happened
. . . You know? How could you? . . . Television? . . .
Wally being pushed into a paddy wagon? . . . Dean
Stallings? . . . You saw all that on . . . Oh, Clarence
Cahill. Well, I wouldn't believe anything he said . . .
Or his wife, Charlotte, either. Wally is not the kind of
boy to go around hitting deans! So you just call Cahill
back and tell . . . You're at his place right now? Well,
you can tell him Wally would never do anything to reflect on his Dad's company. (*Lowering her voice.*) You
stay there. And don't let him call any other stockholders.
I'll have Walter call soon as he returns. (*Hangs up, in-
stantly gets a thought, dials.*) Operator! I wish to place
a call to Dean Stallings! . . . Hathaway College. In New
Hampshire . . . And you get him, no matter *where* he is!
This is an emergency involving my son! (*Pinned down
by phone, she tries to reach her precious copy of Spock
and yet not put down the phone. She just about does it
when the operator is back.*) Yes . . . Yes . . . They
said he's *where? Hospital?* . . . Then you just get him
at the hospital! . . . Not allowed to take any calls?
Good God, what happened to him? . . . Oh? Oh, no!!
Never—never mind.

(*Stunned, she hangs up, sinks down on the couch, shakes her head, as behind her,* WALTER *enters, signals to someone Offstage to enter. He does:* WALTER DAVIS, JUNIOR, *bearded, dirty, stained and streaked, a typical college-type protester.*)

WALTER. (*Crosses* R. C.) Norma! Look what I found!

(*She turns, doesn't recognize him at once, till:*)

WALLY. (*Enters to* C.) Mother?

NORMA. My baby! (*She rushes to him, to kiss him, but there is that beard.*)

WALTER. Keep searching. You'll find a place to kiss. (*She finally does. During it:*) We sent them a fine-looking boy, valedictorian, first in his class. And look what they send back.

NORMA. (*Not releasing* WALLY, *but to* WALTER.) It was *your* idea to let him pick a college way up in New Hampshire, so I wouldn't be visiting him all the time!

WALTER. Somehow, I don't think everybody in New Hampshire looks like *that.*

NORMA. (*She glares at* WALTER, *turns her warmth and attention to innocent, pure victimized son.*) Wally, what did they do to you?

WALLY. Nothing, Mother, nothing, really.

NORMA. They put you in jail!

WALLY. Oh, yeah, that. Well—

NORMA. How long were you *in* that *filthy* place?

WALLY. It's a new jail. Air conditioned.

NORMA. I don't care! They had no right! (*Beat.*) *Did* they?

WALLY. Now, Ma, don't take it so big!

NORMA. You're the first member of this entire family who has ever been in jail!

WALTER. Even her brother Harry was never in jail. (NORMA *greets that with the proper resentment.* WALLY *crossing to chair* R., *unslings guitar from his shoulder and puts it on chair.*) Maybe we were overdue. Statistically speaking, we're way below the national average.

NORMA. How did you get out?

WALLY. (*Crosses back to* NORMA.) Phi Kappa put up their fraternity house as bail!

WALTER. My, isn't that touching!

WALLY. You see, we're going to fight this together. The CCA—

WALTER. Which government are *they* with?

WALLY. Committee for Campus Action. We formed it to make the most of the protest possibilities. CCA strategy is to have us away from Campus so that the impact of our presence isn't used up while *they're* fighting out the legal aspects. That's why I'm here.

WALTER. (*"Legal" makes him interrupt.*) *Legal* aspects? What the hell is going on? Did the school take any action against you?

WALLY. There's talk of being expelled, but it's too early—

WALTER. (*Interrupting.*) Expelled?

NORMA. (*To keep the peace.*) Walter, you just go get the milk.

WALTER. Yes, mam.

(*As* WALTER *turns to go,* WALLY *says:*)

WALLY. And while you're at it, Dad, would you pick up about six dozen cans of beer? (WALLY *crosses behind sofa.*)

NORMA. Six *dozen?*

WALLY. Well, Mother, I'm not exactly alone.

NORMA. Just what *are* you *exactly?*

(WALLY *raises a hand to her to indicate "just a moment and I'll show you." He goes to window and calls out.*)

WALLY. Come on in, fellows! (*Into the room come*

THREE COLLEGE PERSONS. SCOTT, *a tall, scroungy bearded one, in dirty jeans, desert boots, dirty 1914 Army coat, Australian campaign hat, with a flower resting on one ear. Second is* WOODY JACKSON, *a Negro boy, clean shaven, with steel-framed glasses, but as dirty and disheveled as* SCOTT. *And third is* CINDY, *a girl, but, in her pea jacket and European-type cap, which covers her hair, she is indistinguishable from the others.* NORMA, *stunned, looks to* WALTER *who looks back, shrugs.* WALLY *with pride and loyalty.)* Mother! Meet the Group! We're all in this together!

(THE GROUP *acknowledges* MOTHER *with gestures, smiles, etc., but* NORMA *has trouble returning the compliment. She can only ask:*)

NORMA. Together? Isn't that nice. In *what* together?
WALLY. The best way to explain is—

(*He makes a gesture to the* GROUP *and they exit to return almost at once, each with a picket sign.* WOODY *brings in two and gives one to* WALLY. WOODY'S *reads: THERE ARE NO DIRTY WORDS, ONLY DIRTY MINDS.* SCOTT'S *reads: LSD. BETTER LIVING THROUGH CHEMISTRY.* CINDY'S *reads: BACK UP YOUR RIGHT TO SHACK UP.* WALLY *holds one which reads: POT? WHY NOT?* WALTER *and* NORMA *are appalled.*)

NORMA. Wally! Shack up? LSD? Pot? Are you telling us that *you—?*
WALLY. The question isn't *do* I? It's do I have a *right* to! It's a matter of personal freedom!
WALTER. Which includes the right to go to jail, I suppose.
WALLY. (*Embarrassed in front of his cool* FRIENDS.) Now, Dad, let's not make a big flap over this.
WALTER. Wally, make a flap!

SCOTT. (*Crosses down; sarcastically, to* WALLY.) I told you but you kept insisting, "We'll crash at my home for a few days. My folks'll understand." Yeah, man! I should have gone home to California. Might as well get to the nitti gritti.

WALTER. The what?

SCOTT. Nitti gritti—crux, man, crux!

WALTER. (*To* NORMA.) Till this moment I never realized what a beautiful word "crux" was. Wally, whatever you *call* it, get *to* it!

(SCOTT *crosses to chair* R. *and sits.*)

WALLY. Dad, do you have any idea what they tried to do to us?

NORMA. (*To* WALTER.) There! I knew it wasn't Wally's fault! (*To* WALLY.) What *did* they do to you, son?

WALLY. Closed down Radio Free America!

WALTER. Radio Free *Europe,* I heard of that. But Radio Free *America?*

WALLY. *My* station!

WALTER. Your station?

SCOTT. Underground, man, underground.

WALTER. An illegal station? Wally!

WALLY. It's the only way we can get freedom of expression on campus. How else could we defend people like Mike Sanford and his roommate?

WALTER. And just who the hell is Mike Sanford that *you* have to defend him?

WALLY. (*To* WALTER, *as though explaining to a child.*) For the last semester, Mike Sanford and his roommate have been living at this place right off campus. Till one day in English Lit his roommate turned in this paper about Mike.

SCOTT. Sheer poetry. Groovy. Shakespeare.

NORMA. Did Mike know his roommate *felt* that way about him?

WALLY. Of course, Mother. He feels the same way about her.

NORMA. *Her?*

WALTER. You mean those two kids were living together, unmarried, right at school?

SCOTT. What do you think *that* means? (*Referring to posters.*)

WALLY. Scott, cool it. (*To* WALTER.) Her paper was so beautiful, so expressive, so free, real, true and earthy in its Anglo-Saxon simplicity that her English Prof decided to submit it to the Lit Quarterly.

WOODY. And they published it!

WALLY. Whereupon, now hear this for nerve, the Dean decides to censor the whole issue!

WALTER. (*Sarcastically.*) I don't understand why.

NORMA. Wally, continue!

WALLY. Of course, I immediately opened the microphones of Radio Free America. She reads her paper on the air! (WALLY *crosses* U. R.)

SCOTT. And was that girl ever in gear! When she described their sexual relationship—man!

NORMA. She described—the whole thing?

WALLY. Almost!

WALTER. Almost?

WALLY. (*Crosses back to* D. R.) That's when the FCC broke in and confiscated my transmitter!

WALTER. It was about time! Hooray for the Federal Communications Commission!

WALLY. Dad, that girl's civil rights were being violated! So we had to resort to mass protest. I composed a song to symbolize our fight for freedom of all forms of expression.

SCOTT. (*Rises.*) And sang it. Right at the foot of the founder's statue. That's where it's *at,* man!

WALTER. Where what's at?

SCOTT. (*Confronts* WALTER.) The action! And the *inter*action! The abrasive friction of skin against skin. Idea against idea!

(*During above,* SCOTT *advances toward* WALTER *drama-*

*tizing his words by rubbing the flat of his hands to-gether.* WOODY *leans on arch* R. CINDY *sits on step.*)

WALTER. (*Having taken up the gesture.*) When I was a Boy Scout we did that with two sticks.

WALLY. (*To protect* SCOTT, *who is shocked by such barbaric references.*) Dad, please! Don't talk that way to Scott. Show a little respect! (*Arm proudly around* SCOTT.) *He* was expelled from Berkeley!

WALTER. (*Across to* NORMA.) A dropout, cum laude.

(SCOTT *crosses to chair* R.)

WALLY. As we were singing, a crowd began to gather. Must have been at least a thousand—

SCOTT. (*He takes pack off and puts it on floor* R. *of chair, then sits.*) Two thousand, including Faculty and townies.

WALTER. (*Sarcastically proud.*) All gathered to watch my son get arrested! Just what kind of song *was* it?

SCOTT. You have to get it in context. It was out of sight, man, out of sight!

WALTER. Well bring it *into* sight!

CINDY. (*Rises.*) The best way is to sing it.

WALTER. Good God, it's a girl! (WALLY *takes guitar from* SCOTT *as the* FOUR *group into singing formation and start number.*) Oh, we're going to have a recital.

(WALTER *sits on sofa* L., *Downstage end.* NORMA *sits on Upstage end.* WALLY *sits on pouf.* WOODY *on floor with bongos.* CINDY *at* C., *dancing.* SCOTT *stands* D. L., *confronting* WALTER.)

GROUP. (*Sings.*)
        They ain't no dirty words.
        They is just dirty minds.
        They ain't no dirty words.
        They is just dirty minds.

> Who said love is clean and pure?
> How can everybody be so sure?

> What if the word for love was luck?
> What if the word for love was—?

WALTER. (*Rises, horrified; he interrupts.*) Don't you dare! Don't you dare! Not in front of your mother!

WALLY. (*Abashed by such outrageous conduct on the part of his* FATHER.) Sorry, guys. Scott—

SCOTT. (*Intolerantly tolerant.*) It's all right. I understand. After all, he's a father.

WALTER. (*To* WALLY.) You're apologizing for *me?* I work like a dog to send you to one of the best colleges in the East. Why? So you can shack up? Or learn to use filthy language that you could have learned right here at home? And then you have the unmitigated gall to come back and sing that vulgar thing in front of your mother.

NORMA. (*Rises.*) Walter, please, you're being very unreasonable.

WALTER. Are you sticking up for this boy? Okay! Wally, your mother would like to hear the end of your fine song. And all the fine words in it.

GROUP. (*Singing.*)

> Who said love is clean and pure?
> How can everybody be so sure?

> What if the word for love was luck?
> What if the word for love was—
> (*Beat pause, then the sign-off.*)
> End of song!

WALTER. (*Suspecting he's been tricked.*) Now, wait a minute! What did you do there? Wally! I want an explanation!

WALLY. That's the song, Dad.

WALTER. The whole song? You didn't leave anything out?

WALLY. No, Dad.

NORMA. There! You see!

WOODY. Dirt is in the minds of the people.

SCOTT. (*Advancing on* WALTER *to deliver the last of this right in his face.*) You see, sir, we feel that our trouble comes not from what *we* do. But from a decadent, dirty-minded older generation.

WALTER. (*Frustrated, it's either kill* SCOTT *or reply with a non-sequitur.*) Don't you ever get a haircut? Why must you all wear your hair so long?

SCOTT. Why must you all wear yours so short?

WALTER. So we can tell the girls from the boys!

SCOTT. (*He crosses around Upstage and back to sofa, sits.*) We have other ways, sir.

(WOODY *crosses behind sofa, sits on back of it.*)

WALTER. Now, Wally! I want to know exactly what you did that led to your being put in jail!

WALLY. (*Rises, crosses to* DAD.) Well, Dad, believe me, nothing really—

(CINDY *crosses to pouf, sits.*)

NORMA. (*She can't hold back now.*) It had to be something for Dean Stallings to end up in *traction!*

WALTER. In traction?? Dean Stallings?

NORMA. (*Confessing.*) I called when you were out. He's in the hospital.

WALTER. (*To* WALLY.) How did Dean Stallings wind up in traction?

WALLY. We were having this protest and singing our song.

CINDY. Wally's song!

WALTER. Are you sure she's a girl?

WALLY. I wouldn't be engaged to a boy!

NORMA. *Engaged?*

WALTER. Why not? He's a sophomore. Now, get to Dean Stallings!

(NORMA *sits on chair* L.)

WALLY. We stood at the foot of founder's statue, expecting Dean Stallings to show up so we could make our demands. But he didn't. So we had to execute Plan X.

WALTER. Something you learned from the CIA?

SCOTT. *I* created Plan X. Based on my extensive experience at Berkeley and Dartmouth.

WALTER. Berkeley *and* Dartmouth?

WALLY. Plan X called for us to invade the Administration Building, block off the entrance with a wall of bodies and confront Dean Stallings right in his own office.

SCOTT. To make our demands face to face!

WALTER. What demands?

WALLY. No censorship of any college publication!

SCOTT. Representation on the Board of Governors!

WALTER. *You* want to help run the college?

SCOTT. What are you, a *Fascist?*

WALTER. You might as well decide what to teach and how to teach it!

SCOTT. Exactly! Control of the curriculum! Our third demand!

WALTER. Just *one* demand like that could put a dean in traction!

WALLY. Of course, first we had to keep the Kampus Kops out long enough to make the dean listen.

SCOTT. So while the Kops were peeling bodies away from the entrance, we barricaded ourselves in the Dean's office! Built a wall of furniture against the door! That kept the Kops out while we could force the Dean to negotiate.

WALTER. Forcing is not negotiating! I wouldn't blame him if he didn't even listen.

WALLY. Oh, he had to. I had this handcuff on my left wrist. And I snapped the open cuff on Dean Stallings and swallowed the key! So he had—

NORMA. (*Interrupting.*) You swallowed that dirty key? With all the stomach virus that's around. Oh, Wally!

WALTER. We'll get to his stomach later. What about Dean Stallings?

SCOTT. That's when the riot broke out.

WALTER. Riot? You caused a riot?

SCOTT. The Kops tried to force the students away from the entrance. Naturally, the students resisted.

WALLY. Then the Kops broke into the Dean's office, grabbed us both and tried to pass us over the heads of the crowd, handcuffed together. They were in such a hurry to get us into the paddy wagon they dropped him. (*Then.*) The paddy wagon. That's where they used the hacksaw to cut off our handcuffs.

NORMA. Hacksaw? Did they hurt you, Wally?

WALTER. Of course not, Norma. The Supreme Court made a ruling. In a case like that they have to give a general anesthetic. (WALTER *crosses* L.)

NORMA. You mustn't pay any attention to your father when he gets into one of his over-dramatic moods.

WALTER. (*Crossing to* C.) Or any other time for that matter! Why should anyone listen to me? I'm just an idiot running a million dollar business. Mother, did you hear me?

SCOTT. Man, he has lost his cool completely.

WALTER. Young man, you haven't seen cool lost yet. We are going to have a little action around here. And a little interaction. You're going to find out where it's at, man! Wally!

WALLY. Dad, we were only exercising our right of protest!

WALTER. And about Dean Stallings' right? Not to be handcuffed? And not to wind up in traction?

WALLY. Now, look, Dad—

(WALTER *crosses* D. R.)

WALTER. Protest is one thing. But you keep exercising your rights that way and we'll have anarchy. No wonder they put you in jail! Well, Wally, you and your dear

Group will get into my car. And I will drive you back to school. Where you will all apologize to Dean Stallings. (WALTER *crosses back* U. L.)

(CINDY *rises*.)

WALLY. And undermine our whole protest! Oh, no!

CINDY. (*Confronts* WALTER.) We couldn't possibly apologize, sir!

WALTER. I'm talking to my son, if you don't mind.

(CINDY *backs away*.)

WALLY. (*Puts arm around* CINDY.) Please, Dad, don't talk that way to Cindy.

NORMA. (*Aside; still on chair* L.) Good Housekeeping says one of the worst things you can do is antagonize your future daughter-in-law. They never forget.

WALTER. I don't give a damn whether she forgets or not.

NORMA. Wally, you know your father doesn't mean that. He's just a little upset.

WALTER. Norma! Don't explain me. (*To* GROUP.) Now, are you all going to get into my car or do I have to carry you out, one by one?

SCOTT. (SCOTT *rises, confronts* WALTER.) Mr. Davis!! One of the first rules of diplomacy is, never force an issue without leaving yourself a graceful means of retreat. My father's mistake when I was expelled from Michigan.

(WALLY *on step of landing Upstage*.)

WALTER. Michigan, too? Well, I do not intend to retreat. Gracefully or otherwise. Wally?

WALLY. (*Crosses down to* WALTER.) Dad, we are not going back!

WALTER. (*Removing coat; hangs it on back of chair* L.) All right! I wasn't a sergeant in the army for nothing!

NORMA. Walter! Don't you dare!

WALTER. Norma, tonight I am going to dare all those things you have kept me from daring for the last twenty years!

NORMA. Walter, I absolutely forbid you!

WALTER. When my son is wrong, he's going to *admit* he's wrong! In public where he disgraced himself . . . Now, Wally, you— (*Pointing in turn to* WALLY, CINDY, SCOTT, WOODY.) you—you and you—

WOODY. You lay a hand on me and you'll be picketed till the day you die!

NORMA. That's right, Walter, there's a Federal *law* about *him!*

WALTER. Well, law or no law, all four of you are going to get into that car. Peaceably or otherwise. Regardless of race, creed or color!

(*DOOR CHIMES sound.*)

NORMA. (*Rises. Moving to answer.*) Oh, dear.

WALTER. I'll answer that! Probably another reporter. Now, all of you, take your junk into the dining room! Out! All of you! I have to be very careful how I handle this. Public relations, you know! (*During above,* NORMA *and* GROUP *clear to take things and exit to dining room,* R. *DOOR CHIMES.*) Just a moment. Be right there! (*He goes* U. L. *to answer the front door.*) Oh, Clarence! Hello. Come right in. (*As* BOTH *enter.*) Just happened to be in the neighborhood, I suppose. (*They come to* C.)

CAHILL. You know exactly why I'm here, Davis! Where is he? Did he get here yet?

WALTER. Did who get here? What are you talking about?

CAHILL. (*Crosses* L. *to sofa.*) That beatnik, hippy, trouble-making rioting son of yours, that's what I'm talking about.

WALTER. My son is none of your damned business.

CAHILL. (*Crosses back to* WALTER.) It's not only my

business, it's the business of every stockholder when your son destroys the reputation of Weathervane Industries Incorporated!

WALTER. If you're referring to that little campus caper, it had nothing to do with the company.

CAHILL. Oh, didn't it? Well, not only did I catch a glimpse of it on the TV news, but I've gotten calls from four important stockholders this evening. As far away as Boston and New Hampshire. Two of them threatened to unload their stock at the market opening tomorrow. (BOTH *are at* C.)

WALTER. You're exaggerating!

CAHILL. (*Crosses* L. *to sofa, sits.*) Am I? Ask your brother-in-law Harry. He was at my house discussing the whole thing when one of the calls came in.

WALTER. What the hell was Harry doing at your house?

CAHILL. I had him come over. He tried to get you, but you were out. Norma promised you'd call back, but, of course, you never did.

WALTER. (*Calls.*) Norma! She never told me. Norma! Probably forgot to give me the message, that's all . . . *Norma!* (*But she's on, by this last call, from* U. R.) Oh. Why didn't you tell me Harry called?

NORMA. (*On landing,* R.) Good evening, Clarence. I'm sorry I forgot to tell Walter that Harry called. Walter, Harry called.

(*She starts to exit* R., *but* CINDY *comes out and* CAHILL *gets a glimpse of her before* NORMA *shepherds her out.* BOTH *exit* R.)

WALTER. (*Brushing off* CINDY'S *appearance.*) Well, that settles that.

CAHILL. Just what do you call *that?*

WALTER. Oh. Oh, Norma is interviewing a new handman.

CAHILL. (*Rises, crosses to* WALTER.) My attorney says you can be held personally responsible to all the stockholders for destroying the company's most valuable asset. Its name.

WALTER. I know my son and he would never do anything to reflect on my company.

CAHILL. And I say you're lying.

WALTER. You're just trying to blow this up into an issue to take to the stockholders next week.

CAHILL. Next week? I have my attorneys working on this right now. They'll be in touch with every stockholder the first thing in the morning. We'll prove you're lying. (*He starts to go* U. L.)

WALTER. Just a minute, Clarence! (*Grabs* CAHILL *by the sleeve.*) We'll see who's a liar. Wally! Come in here! I brought up my son to give straight answers to straight questions. We don't lie around here. You'll find that out.

(*They cross Downstage.* WALLY *enters from dining room,* U. R.)

WALLY. Hi, Mr. Cahill.

WALTER. Son, in all this—this mess, did you or any of you involve my company?

WALLY. (*Crosses Downstage.*) Why should we? The protest was about freedom, Dad.

WALTER. You didn't refer to the company in any interview or on television?

WALLY. Absolutely not!

WALTER. There! Now, are you satisfied?

CAHILL. I wouldn't take the word of this filthy, disreputable-looking protestor, this jailbird, as far as I could smell him.

WALTER. (*Taking off coat and bearing down on* CAHILL.) That does it, Cahill. You're not going to talk that way about my son!

CAHILL. Now, don't get physical, Walter!

WALTER. Oh, I'm going to get physical. I'm going to help you out of here!

(*The loud voices bring on the* GROUP *and* NORMA *from*

U. R., *ready to find out what's going on or to protect* WALTER *if he needs protection, which he does not.* CINDY *by library.* SCOTT *on landing* L., WOODY *on landing* R.)

NORMA. Walter?

CAHILL. (*Spies the shaggy* GROUP.) Good God!

NORMA. (*Embarrassed by* CAHILL'S *reaction.*) Mr. Cahill—meet the Group.

CAHILL. I've already met them on television. Now, I remember *that* one particularly— (*Pointing out* CINDY.)

WALTER. Oh, the handyman.

CAHILL. Handyman, hell! When your fine son was being shoved into the paddy wagon, that little boy there was holding on to his free arm.

NORMA. That little boy there happens to be our future daughter-in-law.

CAHILL. Whatever it is, she happened to be wearing something had the company's name on it.

WALTER. Now, you're being ridiculous!

CAHILL. Oh, am I? I tell you she was wearing something with the name Weathervane Industries on it—

WALLY. Oh, my god!

WALTER. Wally! What is it?

WALLY. Well, Dad, we have this singing group and when we needed a name, I—well—

(*He signals* CINDY, WOODY *and* SCOTT *who open their jackets to reveal on their sweatshirts the name, THE WEATHERVANES.*)

CAHILL. The Weathervanes!

WALTER. Wally! Why didn't you tell me?

WALLY. I never realized . . . and it's such a good name for a singing group.

WALTER. It also happens to be the name of my company!

CAHILL. *Our* company, if you don't mind! Well, we'll

see what the stockholders say about *that!* (*He exits* U. L., *with* WALLY *in pursuit*.)

WALLY. Mr. Cahill, Dad didn't know anything about it. I just picked the name because it's the first one that came to mind. Mr. Cahill!

(*Onstage,* WALTER *moves to a chair and drops into it, struck dumb by the events of the last sixty seconds.* NORMA *moves to him, consolingly.*)

NORMA. Walter . . . Walter, is there anything I can do?

WALTER. Why, yes, Norma, dear. Look up and see what Spock says about disaster!

*CURTAIN FOR END OF SCENE*

## ACT ONE

### SCENE 2

THE PLACE: *The same.*

THE TIME: *The next morning, early.*

AT RISE: NORMA'S *precious room is alitter with empty beer cans, sweatshirts draped on fine-fabric-ed chairs,* SCOTT'S *digger hat is on* WALTER'S *antenna. Two empty pizza cartons are on two of* NORMA'S *prize chairs.* WALTER *and* NORMA *are seated on opposite sides of the Stage, numb and glum after the events of the past twelve hours.* WALTER *seated on pouf* D. R. NORMA *seated on sofa* L.

NORMA. I still don't understand. What did we do wrong?

WALTER. I kept asking myself that all night long. I think I know.

NORMA. You do?

WALTER. My mistake was not getting killed in combat.

NORMA. (*Looking around the room.*) Look at this place. It's like an invasion. We've raised a generation of intellectual barbarians.

WALTER. (*A sudden decision.*) Norma, I'm going to have to talk with that boy! Soon as he gets up. What time did they go to bed?

NORMA. They turned off the hi-fi after four.

WALTER. (*Consults wrist watch.*) It's only eight-thirty.

NORMA. Are you going to the office?

WALTER. How can I?

NORMA. Oh, Walter.

WALTER. (*Rises, crosses to* NORMA. *Trying to brave it out.*) This—this may be a blessing in disguise. I can be my own boss again. I can start all over, in a little loft and work up. Without Harry. (*She casts a glance.* WALTER *sits chair* U. L.) Okay, I'll take Harry in. I just won't listen to him, that's all. And we'll be free of Cahill. That financial scavenger. Can't build a thing himself. Never earned a dollar on his own. Just because he married money, he circles over businesses other men have built and pounces when he has enough shares of stock in his claws.

NORMA. And Charlotte, trying to buy her way into every club, every charity—

WALTER. Did you ever notice, he even looks like a vulture. (*The PHONE rings.*) My God, he must have this place bugged. Don't answer it.

NORMA. You don't even know if it is Cahill. (*PHONE rings.*) We can't just let it ring.

WALTER. You're right. Tear it out by the roots.

NORMA. Walter, we have to maintain our sanity. (*Answers the phone.*) Hello . . . Oh, Millie! (*Which doesn't delight* WALTER; *he rises and crosses to window* L.) You heard the radio this morning . . . Six o'clock news . . . Seven o'clock news . . . Eight o'clock news.

WALTER. Good coverage.

NORMA. Oh, no, *I* was going to call *you*. Millie, when

you had that trouble with Arthur last year and you took him to a psychiatrist, what did he say? . . . Not Arthur, the psychiatrist . . . No, I just thought that if you told me what he told you, we might apply it to Wally . . . Well, thank you just the same. (*She hangs up.*) She didn't want to tell me. That's Millie. Mean, selfish, stingy, deceitful, evasive, spiteful—

WALTER. That's your best friend you're talking about.

NORMA. You *have* to be her best friend to know her that well.

WALTER. Logical. What did she say? (WALTER *crosses to chair* L.)

NORMA. That they're not the same. Arthur's case and Wally's.

WALTER. (*Sits on chair* L.) I think she's right. Considering Arthur got in trouble selling pornographic pictures.

NORMA. Still she could have told me and let me make up my own mind.

WALTER. To his boy scout troop.

NORMA. Besides, Wally isn't *nearly* as sick as Arthur. (WOODY *enters* R., *hearing this last. Crosses to* C. NORMA, *embarrassed, rises.*) Oh—good morning.

WOODY. (*Smiling.*) Morning. Morning, sir.

WALTER. Morning. (WOODY *is feeling all his pockets as smokers do when they're fresh out.*) Smoke?

WOODY. (*Crosses to* WALTER; *gratefully.*) Please.

WALTER. All we have is cigarettes. (NORMA *and* WALTER *both realize the faux pas. So to cover it, as he offers the cigarette box:*) Filters.

WOODY. (*Taking cigarette.*) Thank you.

WALTER. You're welcome.

(*Conversation is scarce, but then* WOODY *knows from experience that it always is when he's confronted, alone, for the first time, with the parents of his white friends.*)

NORMA. (*Suddenly.*) Uh—breakfast?

Woody. Groovy!

Norma. Anything—uh—special?

Woody. (*Tongue in cheek.*) Grits?

Norma. (*A glance to* Walter.) Well, uh, we don't—uh—

Woody. Chittlins?

Norma. It just so happens we're all out of chittlins. What about some nice fried eggs, bacon, buttered toast and coffee?

Woody. (*Seemingly let down.*) That's what we always have at *home*. I was hoping for something different.

(Norma *starts out, then stops, turns to* Walter *as she realizes she's been put on. Then she exits* U. R. Woody *crosses* R. *to chair* R.)

Walter. (*Ill at ease with* Woody.) Uh—you—you and Wally are fraternity brothers, h'mm?

Woody. Uh-huh.

Walter. You like it? The college, I mean.

Woody. Pretty good, as colleges go. (Woody *turns* R.)

Walter. (*Defensively and proudly.*) *We* think it's one of the best in the east!

Woody. (C. *Simply, yet pointedly.*) So do "we."

Walter. (*Realizing what he said, he becomes apologetic about it.*) By we I meant we White Plains people.

Woody. Just cool it, Mr. Davis, you're too tense. And I've got enough to be tense about as it is. Mind if I use your phone?

Walter. No, not at all.

Woody. (*Starts to cross to phone, stops.*) Long distance.

Walter. Go right ahead. Just so the phone is kept busy.

Woody. Thanks. (*Dials 211.*) Operator . . . Poplar 2-6549. Area Code 312. I want to talk to Mrs. William Jackson. *Mrs.*

Walter. Mother?

Woody. Yes, sir.

WALTER. Long as we're waiting, tell me something. Do you *really* go round calling all white men "Charlie"?

WOODY. Uh-huh—if they're named Charles. (WALTER *nods intelligently, till he realizes he's been put on too.* WALTER *rises, crosses to chair* R., *sits and pretends to read newspaper.*) Ma? It's me . . . I'm all right . . . I'm all right . . . Ma, believe me, I'm all right! What about Dad, did he . . . Oh he *did?* Well, you can tell him . . . Still home? Sure, I'd like to talk to him. But I'm calling on someone else's phone, long distance, and it's expensive . . . Maybe I better *not* talk to him.

WALTER. (*All fathers stick together.*) Take your time!

WOODY. (*Trapped, he has no choice.*) Okay, Ma, put him on . . . Hello, Da— (*He jumps to his feet at the sound of his father's voice. And he gets the chance to complete very little of what he wants to say.*) Yes, sir. Well, I . . . Yes, sir! . . . No, sir . . . Not to waste time . . . Yes, sir, education, sir . . . Yes, sir, I know how much it costs. . . . Now, look, Dad . . . Yes, sir! I'm all right, sir. I give you my word . . . At the Davis house in White Plains. Honest. (*To* WALTER.) Please, Mr. Davis, would you talk to him?

(WOODY *shakes* WALTER'S *hand. He flinches.* WOODY *sits chair* L.)

WALTER. (*He crosses, takes the phone.*) Mr. Jackson, hi there . . . Yes, Wally's Dad . . . *Physically,* they're fine . . . No, no, no violence. Unless you call handcuffing yourself to the Dean violence . . . No, not your son. *Mine* . . . Well, don't you worry. Before this day is over they'll go back to that school and apologize! . . . I'm sure I'll get them re-admitted . . . Nice to talk to you, too. I'd like to meet *you.* Under happier circumstances. Graduation, perhaps . . . Goodbye. (*He hangs up, turns on* WOODY.) Aren't you ashamed of yourself? He works like a dog to send you to one of the best colleges, let you live in a fraternity house, give you an allowance. Things he never had. (*Crosses* R. C.) And what do you do? I don't blame him for being upset. Waiting home for word about you when he should be on his way to work. They'll probably dock him a day's pay. Might even lose his job. All because of you! (*A quick afterthought.*) Well, you write and tell him if he has any trouble because of this mess, I'll *make* a job for him, at Weathervane. (*Beat pause.*) What kind of work does he do?

WOODY. He's a judge.

WALTER. Oh! Oh. I'm sorry. I thought—

WOODY. (*Rises, crosses* C. *to* WALTER.) What everybody else thinks. Look, Mr. Davis, what do you think *I* think?

WALTER. What?

WOODY. (*Looking around, for privacy.*) You won't tell Wally and Scott, will you?

WALTER. Promise.

WOODY. I didn't want to get involved in any protest.

WALTER. You didn't?

WOODY. I had an early date. I wanted to keep that date. They wouldn't let me.

WALTER. What do you mean, they wouldn't let you? You're a free man.

WOODY. Not if you want to be in.

WALTER. "In"?

WOODY. Especially if you're a Negro. If anybody is marching about anything, you have to join.

WALTER. You mean, you really didn't—?

WOODY. This year alone I have put in two hundred and thirteen miles of marching and picketing that I never wanted to do!

WALTER. You must be very tired. (WOODY *reacts.*) Of the whole idea, I mean. Is it that important to be in?

WOODY. Man, if you're not in, you're out. O-U-T.

WALTER. I see. Scott, I'll bet he's in. I-N.

WOODY. Mr. Davis, Scott is *the innest!*

WALTER. Innest?

NORMA. (*Offstage.*) Woody, breakfast is ready!

WALTER. There you are. (WOODY *starts up to exit and* WALTER *follows to call out.*) Norma, give that poor boy plently of nourishment! (*Starts down, saying to himself:*) The "innest." That's a nice word.

(*The DOOR CHIMES sound.* WALTER *is reluctant to answer.* NORMA *comes rushing on.*)

NORMA. Don't let anyone into this house before I tidy up! (*She explodes into a frenzy of clean-up activity.*)

WALTER. Cahill. And his lawyer. To serve the papers.

(*The CHIMES again.*)

NORMA. The girls! It's the girls! I completely forgot my committee meeting.

WALTER. Cahill! *Your* meeting isn't till ten.

NORMA. Do you think they can wait that long? With Wally to gossip about? God, what a day this is going to be!

WALTER. (*Moves to her, comforts her.*) Now, Norma, remember, you're the president. A little dignity. (*The CHIMES again.*) I'm coming, Clarence!

NORMA. You don't even know if it is Cahill.

WALTER. That's right. I'll make a preliminary investigation.

(*He crosses to window.* NORMA *tidies up hastily. He turns back.*)

NORMA. So it isn't Cahill.

WALTER. No. But you're close.

NORMA. Who is it?

WALTER. His wife.

NORMA. Charlotte?

WALTER. The female David Susskind. (*He moves up and toward the entry hall to call.*) Charlotte—please?

(CHARLOTTE CAHILL *enters* U. L. *She is most menacing when she is smiling. And she is smiling this morning.*)

CHARLOTTE. Walter, darling! (*She holds out her cheek for* WALTER *to kiss. Then she heads for* NORMA, *like a mourner at a funeral.*) Oh, Norma, *darling,* I'm so sorry about everything!

NORMA. Thank you, Charlotte, *darling.*

WALTER. (*Watching the* TWO WOMEN *seem to embrace and kiss but never touch, and revolted by the phoney sweetness of it all.*) If anybody calls me, I'll be up in the darling. (*He exits up stairway.*)

(CHARLOTTE *crosses to* L. C., *stands front of chair* L., NORMA *to her* R.)

CHARLOTTE. Well, Norma, darling, I guess we *do* have to talk about it. The meeting, I mean.

NORMA. (*At* C.) Don't you think we should wait for the rest of the committee?

CHARLOTTE. Oh, *that* meeting? *I* was referring to the meeting of the Ad Hoc Committee.

NORMA. (*Suspiciously.*) Ad Hoc Committee?

CHARLOTTE. Late last night. In an emergency, you have to have an Ad Hoc Committee. You remember when we took a position on Viet Nam? Well, when the news about Wally came over TV, naturally we *had* to take a posture.

NORMA. I don't see why Wally is club business.

CHARLOTTE. (*Crosses to sofa, sits.*) The title of your speech was to be, "Successful Child Raising in a World in Transition."

NORMA. (*Crosses to chair* L., *sits.*) Was to be?

CHARLOTTE. It was suggested that you change your title to *"Parent Failure* in a World in Transition."

NORMA. Oh, was it?

CHARLOTTE. (*She rises, crosses back of chair to* R. *of* NORMA.) Norma, darling, our commitment being in the mainstream of current establishment thought, Wally's revolt creates a credibility gap. As to your expertise in child-raising, I mean.

NORMA. I see.

CHARLOTTE. So *we* had to make an agonizing re-appraisal of *our* position. Which called for considerable, meaningful dialogue.

NORMA. Doesn't it always?

CHARLOTTE. Norma, darling, your son was involved in a riot. You, the woman who has for two terms been the head of our power structure. Think what that could do to our club, image-wise.

NORMA. (*She rises, crosses* D. L. *to* R. *of coffee table.*) So you'd rather I didn't speak.

CHARLOTTE. (*Follows, applying the knife subtly.*) Actually, the Ad Hoc Committee was more—resignation-oriented.

NORMA. Resignation? Well, you can tell them that I'm regular-committee-oriented!

CHARLOTTE. Oh, dear. I'm sorry there's been a hostility explosion. We were trying to avoid an eyeball-to-eyeball confrontation. That's why we decided to *cancel* your ten o'clock meeting.

NORMA. (*Crosses* R. *to pouf.*) *I'm* the only one who can cancel that meeting!

CHARLOTTE. (*Follows.*) There'll be no one here.

NORMA. Irma . . . (CHARLOTTE *shakes her head.*) Alice . . . (CHARLOTTE *shakes her head.*) Susan—

CHARLOTTE. As far as you're concerned, the thrust of the entire group is toward disengagement.

NORMA. (*One last hope.*) Millie?

(WALTER *starts down stairs.*)

CHARLOTTE. There's not the slightest dichotomy, organ-ization-wise: *Everyone* is negative-oriented.

NORMA. Well, you can just *tell* everyone that I am *not* going to resign! Not without a fight!

CHARLOTTE. Club-wise this can create a great confi-dence gap.

(WALTER *enters* U. R.)

NORMA. Oh, could it? Well, *I* suggest that on your way out you watch your thrust, door-wise!

CHARLOTTE. Well! Talk about a hostility explosion . . .

*(Starts out on landing.* WALTER *and* CHARLOTTE *both on landing.)*

WALTER. And give my regards to Clarence, because we are also *vulture-oriented!*

CHARLOTTE. Well! Around here there is, quite obviously, an etiquette gap! *(She exits.)*

WALTER. *(Crosses down landing steps to* L. *of* NORMA.) Norma, sweetheart, I'm proud of you . . . the way you stood up to her . . .

NORMA. *(Very hurt.)* All of them turned against me. Every single one.

WALTER. Now, sweetheart, it's not the end of the world. *(He moves to embrace her, then in the midst of it, he gets an idea.)* Norma! There's only one way! That boy has *got* to retract and apologize! Get him down here. *(*WALTER *crosses* L. *of chair.)*

NORMA. You know how stubborn he can be. Remember the first time we tried to get him to eat tapioca? There are still spoon marks on the kitchen ceiling.

WALTER. The hell with the kitchen ceiling! Norma, get him down!

NORMA. *(She crosses up on landing.)* But he's sleeping.

WALTER. Get him down!

NORMA. Walter, there's nothing you can say to him now that can't wait a few hours.

WALTER. *I* can't wait a few hours. Now, get him down! *(*NORMA *doesn't move.)* All right! *(He starts for the stairs.* NORMA *blocks his way. He moves around her, she darts faster to get to the foot of the stairs. She stands there like Barbara Fritchie. He cannot pass.)* Okay! Stand there! *(He turns, comes down to the phone, starts to dial.)*

NORMA. (*Curious, she follows, demanding.*) Walter, what are you going to do? You'd better tell me! Walter, when I ask a question, I'm used to getting an answer!

WALTER. (*But he is too busy dialing.*) Hello! Walter Davis, Junior, this is Walter Davis, Senior! Calling long distance, from the den! Now, you get the hell down here right away! (*Slams down the phone.*) Till this moment I haven't been able to think of a single good reason why we ever gave that boy his own phone!

NORMA. Walter, you have to be very careful with him. You know how excitable he can be under pressure.

WALTER. This morning I expect that boy to reach new heights! (WALLY, *followed by* SCOTT, *comes down the stairs,* BOTH *in pajamas, tousled, sleepy, fighting the light of day.* WALTER *crosses* R. *to* C.) Good morning, son. Ah, I see you are accompanied by your eminent counsel. Make yourselves comfortable. (*He extends a gestured invitation to them to be seated.*)

WALLY. (*To* SCOTT.) Crash! (BOTH *flop down, almost in a stupor, on the nearest available furniture.* WALLY *on chair* R. *and* SCOTT *on landing step* R. NORMA *sits on sofa.*)

WALTER. Now, Son, *I* am about to tell you what *you* are about to do!

WALLY. (*Barely able to raise his head.*) Dad, remember what Scott said about the first rule of diplomacy?

WALTER. Diplomacy? Do you know what you've done to this family in the last twenty-four hours? Look around you! Survey the wreckage!

NORMA. Walter, please?

WALTER. Let's start with your mother! At this time yesterday, she was one of the most respected women in this community. President and main speaker of the White Plains Women's Club. A member of the Board of Education. Now, she is a weeping wreck! Look at those eyes! (NORMA *turns away.* WALTER *crosses* R. C.) And you did this. Because you had to have freedom! To shack up! To use dirty words. When I was your age, we shacked up too.

NORMA. (*Horrified.*) Walter!

WALTER. Some of the other fellows did. And *we* used dirty words, too. But we didn't protest. We didn't parade. Or riot! We just *used* them. We didn't need anybody to cheer us on while we did.

WALLY. Look, Dad, I think—

WALTER. We've had enough thinking around here! What we are short of is listening. Just plain listening. And it might help, if every once in a while, you'd just nod your head a little. (WALLY *and* SCOTT *shrug to each other with bored indifference.* WALTER *stands* U. C., WALLY *is on chair* R., SCOTT *sits on step* R., NORMA *on sofa.*) Now, do you realize what you've done to *me?* You have turned a respectable business man into a fugitive. I hardly dare answer the phone, or the front door. A lifetime of work is down the drain. I'm an outcast. Barred from the gates of my own company by my own stockholders. Two days ago they were begging me to run for Mayor of White Plains! Today I wouldn't have the nerve to run for dog catcher. And you did this. You! Look at you! (*Takes another look.*) Come to think of it, yours is the only generation in history that looks neater in their pajamas than in their street clothes! (*Having delivered himself of the indictment, he challenges.*) Now, if you have anything to say for yourself, say it!

WALLY. (*Raises his head, looks to* SCOTT. *They agree, then he turns to* WALTER.) Well, it's pretty obvious, isn't it?

WALTER. (*Completely non-plussed.*) What?

WALLY. What a lousy job your generation did of bringing up my generation.

WALTER. What did you say?

WALLY. I never wanted to make an issue of it, Dad, but as long as you raised the question—

WALTER. Norma, I'm going to kill them. I'm going to kill them both!

WALLY. Of course, Dad, if you're not emotionally equipped to face the facts.

WALTER. (*Crosses to* WALLY.) I'm as emotionally equipped as you are! And I can see what's coming. So, go ahead! Accuse me! Single-handed, I invented the atom bomb! I invaded the Dominican Republic. I started the war in Viet Nam. I am responsible for air pollution. Water pollution. And the population explosion. Go ahead!

WALLY. (*Ignoring* WALTER *and conferring with* SCOTT.) Marked tendency to become over-emotional. Sorry about that.

SCOTT. You think *he's* a case. You should see *my* father.

WALTER. Well, go on, accuse me!

WALLY. (*Far from accusing him, they merely discuss him condescendingly.*) Notice, he also exhibits severe symptoms of collective guilt.

SCOTT. Uh-huh. Without even being accused. Very interesting syndrome.

WALTER. (*He crosses to front of chair* L.) Take your time. Study the X-rays.

WALLY. (*He rises, crosses to* R. *of* WALTER.) Dad, this is serious.

WALTER. You're telling me? Before we're done you're going to renounce this disgraceful episode. And you're going to restore to this family the respect and the reputation we've always enjoyed.

WALLY. (*To* SCOTT.) "Respect" . . . "reputation" . . . so that's it.

SCOTT. Isn't it always?

WALLY. (*He crosses up to* SCOTT *on step.*) What do you think?

SCOTT. I think you owe it to him.

WALLY. The treatment?

SCOTT. The full treatment.

WALLY. Now?

SCOTT. (*He rises, crosses to chair* R., *sits.*) You haven't got a minute to lose!

WALTER. What the hell are you talking about?

(CINDY *enters* R. WALLY *crosses to* WALTER.)

WALLY. Dad, have you ever considered—really considered—your values, habits and beliefs? I mean instead of accepting them because that's the way your father lived. Have you?

(SCOTT *on chair* R., CINDY *front of bookshelf* R., NORMA *on sofa.*)

WALTER. Now, just a minute!

WALLY. (*Overriding him.*) Well, before it's too late, take a good look at yourself. Because the truth is, you show every symptom of being a typical conformity-ridden wreck.

WALTER. Oh, do I? Well, let me tell you—

WALLY. Next thing you're going to tell us is, that we ought to be more like you!

WALTER. You could do worse!

SCOTT. My father's words exactly—the day I was expelled from N.Y.U.

(WALTER *throws up his hands.* WOODY *enters, stands on landing* R.)

WALLY. Dad—the reason you're so up-tight is that you finally realize you've botched up your whole life.

WALTER. Botched up—I didn't hear that. I didn't hear it!

NORMA. Walter Davis, Junior, you will apologize to your father!

WALLY. He said it himself. (*Turning to* WALTER.) Here you are a grown man and you're scared to answer the phone, or open your own front door. Scared to go to your own plant. Scared to face your neighbors. Scared to run for public office. And why? All because your son won't conform. Just take your business. You worked for eighteen years to build it. Yet you've got yourself into a position where they can take the whole thing away from you. *I* don't call that being very *clever*. Do *you*? (WALTER *can't deny it, so he turns, fuming, to* NORMA, *who by gesture pleads with him to control himself.*) And when you're not being victimized by your business, or by the community, you're being dominated by your wife.

NORMA. Wally!

WALLY. (*Crosses* U. L. C.) That's right, Mother. He has completely abdicated his position as husband and father!

WALTER. (*Sits on chair* L.) Norma, would you read a few lines from Doctor Spock?

WALLY. You can't laugh it off, Dad. Face it. You are a woman-dominated, job-ridden, money-oriented, conformity-castrated victim of a situation you yourself created!

WALTER. (*Rises.*) Norma!! Did you hear the kind of language your son is using to his own father? Whatever happened to respect? Why, when I was your age— (*At the sound of that phrase, the* GROUP, *led by* SCOTT, *breaks into a torrent of anguished cries, mainly "He said it again. He said it."*) What's the matter? What did I say? What?

SCOTT. We have a way of dealing with fathers who use that kind of language!

WALTER. What language? Norma, you heard me. Did I say anything dirty? What did I say? All I said was—

(*But he doesn't get a chance to finish because the* GROUP *starts to sing, with* WALLY *playing the guitar.* WALTER *crosses to pouf, sits.*)

GROUP. (ALL *standing; in rhythm arrangement.*)
　　Family, family,
　　Whatever happened to family?
　　When did it start to go to hell? Well . . .
　　The day that Dad, that dear old sage
　　Invented that cliche, when I was your age.

　　There's nothing so sad
　　As dear old Dad

Who lived in those days of yore
No one had it rougher
No one had it tougher
Than dear old Dad.

SCOTT. (*Reciting proudly.*) To hear him tell it, when he was my age, my Dad lived on the same block as Abraham Lincoln. And every day they walked seventeen miles to school together.

CINDY. (*Proudly.*) My Dad worked his way through kindergarten. Selling matches to other children. In the snow.

WOODY. (*Proudly.*) When he was my age, my Dad was a slave on a big plantation. And he lived in a log cabin. Without air conditioning.

WALLY. (*Proudly.*) When he was a boy, my Dad had a paper route—

WALTER. (*Rises.*) Well, I did!

WALLY. At the age of two!

GROUP.

There's nothing so sad
As dear old Dad—

WALTER. (*Interrupting.*) Now, I've heard enough about your Dad, and your Dad, and yours and— (*To* WALLY.) especially yours!!

(GROUP *backs off* U. L.; SCOTT *at* C. WALLY *puts guitar on coffee table and crosses up around sofa.*)

SCOTT. What we are saying, is that we are here, man. And we are going to make a noise. Our own kind of noise. And one thing we are *not* going to do is take the blame for you running out.

WALTER. Running out? Why, I did more for this boy— gave him the best schools, the best camps, I gave him all the things *I* never had!

WALLY. Sure, Dad. But why? Because you loved me? Or because you were trying to buy your way out?

(CINDY *stands behind chair* L.)

NORMA. Don't you dare talk that way to *your* father!

WOODY. It's not just him, Mrs. Davis. My dad! All dads!

SCOTT. You fell so much in love with the almighty dollar, you needed all your time to pursue it.

WALLY. So you turned me over to teachers, specialists, summer camps—which left you free to go right *on* chasing it!

SCOTT. And that's the nitti gritti, baby. Now, as far as I'm concerned, it's back to the sack! (*He exits, going back upstairs.*)

(WALTER, *benumbed by the attack, especially by this first view of how his own son feels about him, turns away, drops onto pouf deeply hurt.* NORMA *takes over.*)

NORMA. Wally, *I* think you'd better talk to your father!

(*She gestures* WOODY *and* CINDY *out. They exit. She takes one last concerned look at* FATHER *and* SON *and exits. There is a quiet, tense moment.*)

WALLY. (*Crosses to* WALTER.) Dad, I'm sorry. (WALTER *looks up, expectantly awaiting an apology but instead:*) Not for what *I* said. But because *you* misunderstood.

WALTER. I always thought my son loved me, respected me.

WALLY. (*Gets on left knee* L. *of pouf.*) Dad, it's possible to love someone—and still *not* love everything they do.

WALTER. (*Touched by what his* SON *said; he looks up conceding.*) Maybe *I* was too tough on *you*, before.

WALLY. (*Conceding.*) I guess by your standards you had a right to feel outraged.

WALTER. It's not my standards or my good I'm worried about. It's you, son. One disgrace like this on your record can affect your whole life. Keep you out of the right professional school. Or the right job. You're going to marry that—that girl—have children . . . You have to be prepared to support them. You've got to think of your place in the scheme of things.

WALLY. (*Rises.*) Up at school, that's all we *do* think about, Dad. "The scheme of things." And our place. *And we don't like it!* (WALTER *reacts.*) So we have to find our own way. Just as you found yours.

WALTER. Sure. But we never did the kind of thing your generation does. Why, when I was your— (WALLY's *reaction stops him.*) Okay. I won't say it. (*Then can't resist.*) But we didn't!

WALLY. We have our own ideals. And our own heroes.

WALTER. Like Scott, I suppose. Collector of Colleges!

WALLY. (*Moves table down and sits on it next to pouf.*) Don't put him down, Dad. So he's been kicked out of a lot of schools. But did you ever think, he has to be pretty bright to be *admitted* to all those schools?

WALTER. If he'd just find one and settle down!

WALLY. He's searching, Dad. We all are. For the first time, a new generation comes along that doesn't have to worry about where its next meal is coming from, or about a roof over its head. Thanks to *your* generation. So we're taking the time to raise our heads, look around and find out if the world can't be better, more enjoyable, more peaceful. We're searching for new answers. New ways. New ways for everything, Dad! And it's a great search! *Who knows where the answer will be found?* (WALTER *does a take on that.*) A new religion? Maybe. A new form of government. Or mind-expanding drugs. (WALTER *snorts at that one.*) Or love!

WALTER. I've heard all about that! "Love-ins"!

WALLY. What's your alternative, Dad? Hate-ins? (WALTER *bristles.*) Your generation tried hate, war! And failed! We'd like to try love. You gave me a religion that *said,* Love thy neighbor. But then in small type it said, just be choosey who your neighbor is. You handed me a form of government that *said,* All men are created equal. But I only have to look crosstown to see *that* isn't true. You fought two wars to save the world. But it has never been in more danger. Well, *we're* searching for ways to make good on the very standards and values that *you* gave us! Freedom, love, equality! And while we are, we are not going to go round looking like neat, straight, IBM cards with the right holes punched in us! (*Taking a straight, stiff posture.*) Must shave. Wear clean shirt. Get haircut. Do not fold, tear or mutilate. Else we won't fit your big IBM machine called "the scheme of things," which I suppose includes going into your business!

WALTER. I just hate to see you waste the best years of your life making such obvious mistakes!

WALLY. I've got to do my own searching. And make my own mistakes!

WALTER. Oh you're doing that, all right.

WALLY. (*Angrily.*) Now, look, Dad—do I have to spell everything out for you?

WALTER. No, you don't, Son! Now, I think you better join your Group—and go back to the sack! (WALLY *controls his temper, turns, and starts back up the stairs. Almost to himself.*) In, inner, innest . . . so that's the new language, is it? And those are the new ideas? Okay!

(NORMA *enters R., having heard the raised voices, and being concerned, is doubly so when she finds* WALTER *in his strange mood.*)

NORMA. Walter . . . Walter? (*He doesn't answer, but goes to get his cap.*) Where are you going?

WALTER. (*Strangely.*) "Who knows where the answer will be found?"

NORMA. Walter! *Where are you going?*

WALTER. Out. In an "in" sort of way, that is.

NORMA. (*Thinking he's lost his moorings.*) Walter Davis! Just what are you going to do?

WALTER. Norma, I don't know. But I can tell you this. I am no longer going to be a woman-dominated, conformity-castrated wreck! (*He strides off* L. *as:*)

*CURTAIN COMES DOWN*

*END OF ACT ONE*

# ACT TWO

## SCENE 1

THE TIME: *Several hours later.*

AT RISE: *The room is in worse turmoil from the invasion. And in addition there are newspapers which have been opened, read and scattered around.* NORMA *is at the window, searching; then comes away, worried, upset, can't resist picking up one of the newspapers again.*

NORMA. (*Reading line under photo.*) "Riot scene at Hathaway College. With Walter Davis, Junior, local White Plains student, and unidentified boy on his left." God! (CINDY *enters* R.) Oh!

CINDY. Any word yet? (NORMA *shakes her head.*) He never showed at the office? (NORMA *shakes her head.*) Does he do this often? (CINDY *sits on chair* L.)

NORMA. He always used to say, "I've got to set an example for the staff." (*A beat later.*) Good heavens, did I say, "He always *used* to say"?

CINDY. (*She nods gingerly.*) You think he just freaked out? (NORMA *reacts, puzzled.*) Turned off. Did something drastic.

NORMA. I don't know. He's never *done* anything like this before. Even when I subscribed to Lincoln Center.

CINDY. (*A professional observer.*) He's against all culture—

NORMA. He insisted we didn't have time to read all the magazines and go to all the things I already subscribed to. He said the only way he could catch up would be to read the magazines during the concerts. (CINDY *nods sympathetically.*) Do you have the same trouble with Wally?

53

CINDY. Oh, no! Wally is really turned on. Outer-directed, I mean.

NORMA. (*Rising to the defense of her man.*) Walter is too! Only his takes the form of general hostility.

CINDY. (*She rises, crosses to sofa, sits below* NORMA.) We've *studied* cases like him. (NORMA *looks at her resentfully for calling* WALTER *a case.*) Up at college. I'm a psych major.

NORMA. Really! (*Delighted to find another "expert" in the field.*) Uh . . . Cindy . . . (*In a confidential way, she beckons the* GIRL *to sit down.*) What's your given name—Christian name—Lucinda?

CINDY. Cinderella.

NORMA. (*Horrified.*) How could I *possibly* put that on a shower invitation?! (*Recovering from being too obvious.*) I'm sorry.

CINDY. (*She rises, crosses to front of chair* L.) It's all right. Most people react the same way.

NORMA. It *is* rather unusual.

CINDY. Mother and Dad wanted a name that had never been given to any other girl—real girl—before.

NORMA. Non-conformists.

CINDY. (*Nods.*) The first six years of my life it was quite usual for the three of us to go round the house completely naked. All the time.

NORMA. *Was* it?

CINDY. (*She sits on chair* L.) Then suddenly everything changed.

NORMA. Oh?

CINDY. I started to go to the Progressive Schoolhouse. And we had this activity called "Show and Tell."

NORMA. Oh.

CINDY. They put it squarely to my parents. Either they had to wear clothes or I had to leave school.

NORMA. Did you find—in later years, that it all—well, did it affect your outlook on Sex?

CINDY. I don't know.

NORMA. You don't know how you feel?

CINDY. Oh, I know how I *feel*. What I don't know is, how I would feel if I were brought up differently.

NORMA. (*She rises and crosses Upstage of* CINDY *and to her* R. *Nowhere near the answer she expected, but it is logical.*) Yes, yes, I see what you mean. But what *I* mean is . . . do you . . . well, do you—?

CINDY. (*Simply, frankly.*) Don't you really mean, do *Wally* and I?

NORMA. Well—yes—*do* Wally and you?

(CINDY *shakes her head, deliberately.* NORMA *is quite obviously relieved, till:*)

CINDY. (*Leans over to* NORMA.) What's wrong with him?

NORMA. (*Always the defending mother.*) Why there's nothing wrong with Wally! Nothing at all! He's always been a perfectly normal boy. I daresay he's in the upper percentile of his class when it comes to sex. Just as with everything else. (*Beat, then:*) Well, he's certainly not below the middle percentile. (*Beat, then:*) Of course . . .

CINDY. Yes?

NORMA. There *was* that endocrinologist . . . He said that Wally was— (*She stops.*)

CINDY. (*She rises and crosses to* NORMA.) Mrs. Davis, I have a right to know.

NORMA. He said, Wally was a slow developer. Normal. But slow.

CINDY. Oh, he's slow all right. (NORMA *resents that.*) That's not meant as criticism. (*Trying to make up for it.*) He's introspective. Thorough.

(*A noise from the basement-kitchen area makes* NORMA *excuse herself with a gesture and go toward the* U. R. *area to inquire.*)

NORMA. Wally? Are you back? Son! (*A beat, then to* CINDY.) I could have sworn I heard them coming in the back way. (*A second idea makes her call.*) Walter! Is that *you*, Walter? (*There being no answer, she returns to* CINDY.) I'm sorry, dear. But every normal household noise sounds like an explosion today. Where were—? Oh, Wally—being slow.

CINDY. Mrs. Davis, I didn't mean to upset you. But he *is* slow. Sexually, he's what you might call an underachiever.

NORMA. (*Really on the defensive now.*) I can't understand it. We tried to give him a healthy outlook. We always used to discuss sex freely.

CINDY. (*She crosses to behind chair* L., *hands on back of chair.*) Oh, he's very good at *that*.

NORMA. What?

CINDY. Discussing. But when it comes to action—I'm not complaining, you understand.

NORMA. (*Slightly edgy.*) I understand.

CINDY. (*Crosses to* NORMA.) It's just that I'm worried—

NORMA. Wally is absolutely normal!

CINDY. (*Her real basic concern.*) Then what's wrong with *me?*

NORMA. (*Relieved, almost delighted her son is in the clear.*) Yes, there has to be a reason. (CINDY *nods, worried.*) Could it be the way you dress?

CINDY. All the other girls dress this way and you should hear the stories when they come back to the Dorm at night.

(NORMA *looks,* CINDY *becomes immediately silent.*)

NORMA. Have you ever let him—know—how you feel?

CINDY. I've come right out and asked him.

NORMA. (*Woman to woman.*) Oh, now, that's a mistake.

CINDY. It is?

NORMA. Oh, yes. Didn't your mother ever tell you?

(CINDY *turns away* L. *to front of chair.*)

CINDY. My mother never had this problem.

NORMA. (*Crosses* R. *two steps.*) That's true. They sit around naked all the time.

CINDY. They haven't done that in years!

NORMA. I'm glad. Because ever since you mentioned it, I've had this perfectly dreadful picture of three naked people trimming a Christmas tree.

CINDY. We never did that.

NORMA. That's nice.

CINDY. (*A sudden thought.*) Maybe *that's* the trouble.

NORMA. I don't think trimming the tree would have helped.

CINDY. Maybe my telling Wally about my early childhood *did* something to him.

(*Before* NORMA *can answer, a SOUND at the front door interrupts and* WALLY, *followed by* WOODY *and* SCOTT, *come on, breathy and with all the indications of having made an intensive search.*)

NORMA. Wally?

WALLY. We couldn't find him. Went to the plant. The gym. The luncheon club. Even out to the golf club. Nobody has seen him, nobody!

NORMA. Wally! Something terrible has happened to your father!

WALLY. (*Moving to her to comfort her.*) If it had, there'd be a report some place.

NORMA. (*Suddenly.*) Call New York! Lincoln Center!

WALLY. Lincoln Center?

NORMA. Driving back from a concert or a play, he sits there gripping the wheel and muttering, "Some day, Norma, I'm going to burn myself on the steps of Lincoln Center."

WALLY. Dad's the most stable individual I know. He's not going to do anything foolish, or destructive.

(SCOTT *sits on chair* R. WOODY *sits on back of sofa.*)

NORMA. Last night was quite a shock. And the things you said to him this morning! Then the stockholders' fight and the threat of a strike—even the strongest man might crack! That's it, he just cracked! (NORMA *crosses and sits on chair* L.)

WALLY. Not Dad!

CINDY. (*The psych major.*) Has he evidenced a strong sense of insecurity about his business of late?

NORMA. Plus hostility, aggression, general resentment.

WALLY. (*To* SCOTT *and* WOODY.) That's Mom, always available for consultation.

NORMA. (*Silences him with a look, then to* CINDY.) Go on, dear.

CINDY. Fromme says that in middle age that could be a masking symptom for loss of sexual power.

NORMA. I don't think so!

SCOTT. Maybe he hates his business.

WOODY. Maybe he just hates Lincoln Center.

NORMA. (*She rises and crosses* D. R. *to pouf.*) Maybe *we* ought to stop talking about him as if he were a psychiatric case!

WALLY. (*Follows her.*) Mother comes from a very emotional family. (*He puts his arms around* NORMA *to comfort her.*) Of course, it is possible that I—went too far.

NORMA. (*Her first hint.*) Son?

SCOTT. Maybe it was a mistake to blow his mind.

NORMA. Blow his mind? What in the world is *that?* Wally, what did you do to your father? I insist on knowing!

WALLY. It's the frontal attack.

SCOTT. On the entrenched mind, the dug-in, the dogmatic.

CINDY. The ones you can't reason with.

WOODY. Anyone over thirty.

NORMA. I see.

WALLY. You have to face them, head on.

NORMA. (*Helpfully.*) Eyeball to eyeball?

(Woody *crosses up and sits on landing step.*)

WALLY. Right!

SCOTT. You blast every value they hold dear. Material, spiritual, political, sexual.

WALLY. You shake them loose from every belief.

SCOTT. You just "blow their minds" free and clear of every preconceived thought.

NORMA. (*Rises—WALLY pursues.*) So *that's* what you two were doing! And to your own father! (NORMA *circles Upstage, then to window. WALLY follows.*)

WALLY. I only tried to free him from all the decadent concepts that have made him such a selfless conformist. Right now I can see him wandering the streets, shook up, re-examining his whole life, questioning, seeking.

SCOTT. *We* did that once to a philosophy professor at Oberlin.

NORMA. Oberlin, too?

SCOTT. Flipped, flipped out completely.

(ALL *sit in position except* WALLY.)

NORMA. (*Goes to phone.*) Call the police!

WALLY. (*Crosses to NORMA.*) This is something Dad has to face by himself. All *we* can do, in the moment of crisis, is to maintain our perspective, Mother, our cool.

NORMA. (*Crosses to R. C.*) It is very hard to maintain one's cool when one's husband is wandering out there, with his mind—*blown!*

WALLY. (*Sits on chair L.*) Now, Mother—

NORMA. That reminds me. That column in Woman's Day. "Your Husband—Man and Boy." This marriage counselor is always saying, "A man can be successful, even run a big business, but he still needs someone to run him. Underneath, part of him will always remain a boy."

(WALLY *on chair* L., CINDY *on sofa*, SCOTT *in chair* R., WOODY *on back of sofa.*)

CINDY. Advice like that destroys respect for the father image. Which leads to more homosexuality than any other cause.

NORMA. Oh, I don't think so. Why, I've read that column for years and there's been no effect whatsoever—

(*But on the last word she suddenly becomes aware, and* CINDY *becomes aware and they both look at each other, then at* WALLY. *Till it dawns on him too and he explodes:*)

WALLY. Oh, my God! Have you two amateur psychiatrists been working on *me?* (*He jumps up, crosses up to landing, and* CINDY *goes to assuage him.*)
CINDY. Wally, I never—

(*But they are all interrupted by a SOUND Offstage that draws* WALLY'S *attention and he spies Offstage* R.)

WALLY. Dad!
NORMA. Walter, is that you?
WALLY. Now, Mother, he's back. And he's obviously okay. So just relax.

(*She exits right to find out about* WALTER, *and* WALLY *follows.*)

WOODY. You think he did blow his mind—completely?
SCOTT. It's the after-effects we have to worry about.
CINDY. After-effects?
SCOTT. Some of them suffer severe post-operative depression.
WOODY. Flip out and never come back?
SCOTT. Possible.
WOODY. Too bad. He's really a nice guy. For someone over thirty.

(SCOTT *rises, crosses* C.; *expertly.*)

SCOTT. It's the emotional bends. Caused by shooting up too fast from the depths of conformity to the heights of sudden freedom. Puts bubbles in the emotional bloodstream.

CINDY. If anything happens to Wally's dad, it'll be your fault.

SCOTT. Wally started this, when he turned on about that mass protest.

CINDY. (*Rises.*) It was our job to turn him off!

WOODY. All I wanted to do was keep a date. With a girl of my own ethnic group.

(SCOTT *in chair* L.; CINDY *stands to his* R.)

SCOTT. One thing sure, flipped out or shook up, old man Davis'll be a lot easier to deal with from now on. Like my old man.

(NORMA *and* WALLY *return. She is obviously upset by the Offstage happenings. They cross down to easy chair* R.)

NORMA. Slam the basement door in my face, will he? Well! I've seen your father in many moods but I've never seen him like this before. (NORMA *sits chair* R.)

WALLY. (*He stands to her* L.) Ignore him, Mother. Just don't pay any attention to him. Till he comes out of it. Don't *any* of you pay attention to him!

(NORMA *in chair, in an adamant attitude, turned away from the entrance. Behind her,* WALTER *enters. He is dressed in dirty jeans, dirty sweatshirt, and long-haired wig. He carries a placard on a stick, reading "FREE SPEECH FOR PARENTS." The* OTHERS, *including* WALLY, *react but* NORMA *gives them orders.* CINDY U. L.; SCOTT *and* WOODY *at sofa.*)

NORMA. Ignore him! It's the only way!

WALLY. Mother!

NORMA. I don't care what he's done, he— (*She is turning till she sees.*) *Walter Davis!*

WALTER. (*Smiles benignly, exhibits placard.*) Yes, mam?

NORMA. Just what do you think you're doing?

WALLY. Easy, Mother, actually it's kind of funny.

WALTER. Cool is the word, son!

NORMA. (*Rises, crosses to him.*) Cool or not, just what is *that* supposed to mean?

WALTER. (*Brandishing placard.*) Exactly what it says.

NORMA. Walter Davis, you better start making sense!

WALTER. Oh, I make sense, especially to me. It's about *time* we had free speech. Here, hold this! (*Gives placard to* CINDY.)

CINDY. (*Takes placard.*) Free speech for parents?

WALTER. (*To* CINDY.) Higher!

CINDY. (*Holds placard higher.*) Mr. Davis, that's ridiculous!

WALTER. I knew you'd think that! My wife is constantly warning me, "Don't say that, Walter, you'll give him a trauma. You'll scar him for life!" (*To* WALLY.) Well, child, get scarred!

NORMA. You stop that this instant!

WALTER. And if I don't, what'll you do? Report me to Parents' Magazine?

(WALTER *begins to slowly circle Upstage around* R. *to* R. *of pouf.*)

CINDY. I've heard about flipped out. But never anything like this!

WALLY. (*Crosses to* CINDY.) Let him get it out of his system. Maybe he'll hang loose from now on.

WOODY. (*Sits on sofa.*) I just hope *my* father doesn't hear about this!

NORMA. I will not have you talking about your father as though he wasn't here!

WALTER. (*Hopping onto the pouf* D. R.) Because, kiddies, I am here! And this time *I* am the one who is protesting. I think that parents, especially fathers, should have the right to speak out, freely, on any subject. Even on how to bring up their own kids. And I am going to start right now. Walter Davis, Junior, you are a mess. You are a disgrace to every value we've ever tried to teach you. You are an upper middle class bum!

NORMA. (*Crosses right to* WALTER.) Walter! Now, where did you ever get such dirty clothes? Look at those sneakers! Filthy!

WALTER. (*He crosses* R.) Magi-dirt!

NORMA. Magi-dirt?

WALTER. With a secret ingredient.

NORMA. There is no such product as Magi-dirt!

WALTER. Would you like to bet?

NORMA. (*Exploding.*) Walter Davis, you stop that immediately!

WALTER. (*A wounded sprite.*) Please, Norma, you're scarring me.

NORMA. Tell me where you got this Magi-dirt!

WALTER. (*He sits on table near bookshelves* R.) I made it. I mixed some dirt from the vacuum cleaner. Some furniture oil. A little grease from the floor of the garage. Then I needed something to impart aroma. After all, nothing that looks like that— (*Indicating* SCOTT.) can exist without a smell. So I sneaked up to the kitchen and got a big dab of bacon fat. Then I mixed it all together, poured it into the washing machine and put it on Hurry-Up Dirt Cycle.

NORMA. There is no such cycle *on* that machine.

WALTER. There is now.

NORMA. Walter!

WALTER. Then I put it on Hurry-Up Spin Dry, and behold, MR. DIRT. (*He assumes Mr. Dirt pose.*) Here, want to smell?

NORMA. (*Starts* L. *to phone.*) I'm going to call Doctor Miller!

WALLY. (*Rises, stops* NORMA *with speech.*) And let word of this get around the neighborhood?

NORMA. You're right. (*Adopting a different tack toward* WALTER.) Walter, you've scared us half to death. Now, you can just take off those filthy clothes, shower, shave, get into your own clothes and go down to the office! (*Instead of yelling as would have been his custom,* WALTER *just stands there smiling benignly.*) You've got to perfect the new model! (WALTER *is unmoved, but smiling.*) You've got to make plans to defend yourself against that stockholders' suit by Clarence Cahill. Walter, you can't just stand there grinning! (WALTER *is still unmoved or untroubled, so she is forced to plead.*) Walter? Walter, please? Please, change your clothes and go to the office?

WALTER. I like these clothes.

NORMA. (*Exasperated.*) Do you realize how ridiculous you are?

WALTER. Not at all.

NORMA. (*Another sudden pressure.*) Weathervane will go right to hell!

WALTER. I'm sure they have television down there, too. Maybe even underground movies on the late show.

NORMA. Walter, if word of this gets out, you'll *never* be able to stop Clarence Cahill. You'll be out of the company, forever.

WALTER. Oh, I don't want either one of you to worry about your financial security. *I* am going into a new line of business! (*Comes down off pouf, to* NORMA.)

WALLY. (*He crosses* L. *to him.*) You're giving up Weathervane?

WALTER. I'm selling all my stock. And I am going to open a chain of A.P. supermarkets from coast to coast!

NORMA. There already is a chain of A&P supermarkets.

WALTER. A.P. for Angry Parents. And we are going to stock a line of entirely new products. Like Silent Spray!

NORMA. Silent Spray? (*She looks to the* OTHERS, *wondering did they hear the same words.*)

WALTER. It comes in a handy can. With a push-button

top. And whenever a kid says some dirty words, instead of talking to him, or pleading with him, or begging him, you just take up the can and— (*Sound of spray directed right in* WALLY's *face.*) Right in the kisser!

(WALLY *sits on pouf.*)

NORMA. Walter!

WALTER. It has a secret ingredient. SOAP!

WALLY. He's incredible!

SCOTT. Incredible? He's dangerous!

WALTER. For parents with children who are given to kicking, crying, screaming and turning blue, we have a product called Insta-Soothe. This one the harried father sprays into his own ears. And the stuff hardens. So he can just sit there and read his paper without being disturbed by his squealing kid. Or by his wife, laughing at "That's Our Dad."

NORMA. (*Starts for phone.*) Now, I *am* going to call Doctor Miller.

WALTER. Do that! He'll be just in time to see me unveil our new line of Games For Parents. Obliterate the Orthodontist. We are through raising kids with straight teeth and crooked minds!

NORMA. Now, I *have* to call Doctor Miller.

(*As she heads for the phone, he intercepts her with:*)

WALTER. First, you ought to hear about our most recent invention, Trauma-Tize.

SCOTT. "Trauma-Tize"?

WALTER. It is shaped like a doll. A big doll. And it looks like a father. You put it in the child's room and turn it on. And every time the child complains the father doll says, "Shut up!" (SCOTT *pulls back.*) Our labs are on the brink of a breakthrough. They're working on a model that hits. (*He swings,* SCOTT *cringes.*)

NORMA. I won't *call* Doctor Miller! I won't *expose* him to this.

WALTER. Oh, that's too bad. Because he'll miss the world premiere of our most important new product. Rapid-Dad!

NORMA. *Don't anyone ask him!*

WALTER. To be used when the going gets *really* rough. When a kid has his father pinned against the wall with those soul-searching words, "But, Dad, all the other kids have them." For moments like those, Rapid-Dad! In a can. With a pushbutton. But this one has a mirror attached. Because this, the father has to spray on his crumbling spine. (*He goes through motion of spraying, makes the sound, then his face lights up, he seems to grow before our eyes.*) And suddenly, he stiffens. And he's able to say, *no!! It* has a secret ingredient, too. Guts!

SCOTT. Loose is loose, but he's unhinged!

WALTER. Yes, we are going to put an end to over-sensitive children. We are going to pamper over-sensitive parents.

(*The PHONE rings,* NORMA *is delighted to answer.*)

NORMA. Hello? . . . Yes? . . . Oh, thank God. It's your secretary. They've been looking all over for you!

WALTER. (*He advances to phone, takes it, brushes back his wig to free his ear.*) Good afternoon, Miss Dockhouser. And how are you today? . . . Oh . . . Oh . . . he did? Did he now? Well, well, well. Now, Miss Dockhouser, you can just tell my dear brother-in-law Harry to handle Cahill all by himself. Because I am resigning from Weathervane!

NORMA. Wally!

WALLY. (*Jumping up.*) Mother, he's *not* kidding!

WALTER. Yes, Miss Dockhouser, resigning. So you can tell Cahill he can do whatever he wants to with Weathervane, including but not limited to taking it and—

NORMA. Walter!

WALTER. He can do whatever he wants to . . . That's right! (*He hangs up with great finality. Then as he is about to walk away from it, he gets an afterthought. He reaches down, seizes the phone cord and rips it out.*) Take out my instrument, will they?

WALLY. Dad!

CINDY. Mr. Davis!

(*Casually, lightly, freely, he strides away from the phone with* NORMA *following him and pleading.*)

NORMA. Walter, the years you struggled to establish that business. Designing product, selling, thinking up new slogans. Even risking your life to make antenna installations on icy roofs in the very beginning, remember?

WALTER. Old-fashioned nonsense like hard work is a thing of the past. *I* am joining my *son!*

WALLY. (*Crosses to him.*) In what?

WALTER. New times demand new approaches. We've always been used to businesses called "Smith and Son," "Jones and Son," "Davis and Son." Nobody has ever heard of a business called "Davis and Father." But that's no reason why there can't be one. So I am going into my son's business. (*Puts arm around* WALLY.)

NORMA. Your *son's* business?

WALTER. Full time rebelling!

WALLY. Dad!

WALTER. And I am starting out just as I did in the early days, with a few hand-made samples. (*He exits* U. R.)

WALLY. (*Follows him Upstage.*) Hand-made samples! Of what? Davis and Father! Mother?

SCOTT. I've never seen a flip like this! Even with LSD!

WOODY. Keep him away from *my* father!

CINDY. His may be the most blown mind in history!

NORMA. (*She crosses to phone table.*) I'll get Doctor Miller over here right away. He'll give him a sedative and we'll put him to bed! That's what we'll do!

(*But* WALTER *returns, wearing a sandwich sign. And*

*carrying a ukulele, the guitar of his generation. The front sign says: "BACK UP YOUR LOVE WITH THE BACK OF YOUR HAND." He comes down, then turns to reveal the back sign, "DOCTOR SPOCK IS A CROCK." He holds up his uke.*)

WALTER. I found this in the attic. (*He strums.*) I'm working on a new song that gets right to the nitti gritti, man! (*He strums and sings.*)

They ain't no dirty minds
They is just dirty words, *yeah!*

They ain't no dirty minds
They is just dirty words, *yeah!*

Like woman dominated, yeah-yeah.

Money oriented, yeah-yeah.

Father abdicated, yeah-yeah.

Husband castrated, yeah-yeah!

NORMA. Walter! You will stop that, at once!

WALTER. Cool it, baby. You're too tense. Just hang loose. Besides, my public is waiting!

NORMA. Don't you dare leave this house looking like that!

WALTER. Don't try to stop me, baby! (*As he starts out.*) Oh, by the way, son, where would a man make a connection for a few sticks of pot? Never mind. I'll look it up in the yellow pages. Or the Reader's Digest. (*Singing, he exits.*)

They ain't no dirty names
They is just dirty words, yeah-yeah!

*CURTAIN FOR END OF SCENE*

## ACT TWO

### SCENE 2

THE TIME: *Late afternoon, same day.*

AT RISE: NORMA *is looking out of the window to get some sign of* WALTER. CINDY *in* R. *chair, working on a guitar chord.*

NORMA. (*Turning from window.*) I never should have let him leave this house looking like that!

CINDY. You couldn't chloroform him and lock him in the basement.

NORMA. *Why not?*

CINDY. I wish there were something *I* could do.

NORMA. Wally'll find him, I'm sure. Somewhere, somehow. (CINDY'S *plink motivates her to ask.*) Is that what brought you two together? Music?

CINDY. (*Nodding.*) We met at a rally. Wally was singing his very first protest song. It was against War *and* the population explosion. It was called "Make Love Not War But Be Careful."

NORMA. That's a nice title. (*DOOR CHIMES sound.* CINDY *starts for door.*) If that's some reporter, asking about Walter, don't let him in! No, we *have* to let him in. Maybe *he* knows where Walter is! But don't say a word. I'll handle this! (*During above* CINDY *has gone to open the door. Now* CINDY *comes back on staring at a strange* SCOTT, *who enters, eyes fixed and staring as though he's seen the first atomic explosion. He crosses* R., *drops into chair* R., *stunned and unanswering as* NORMA *asks:*) Scott? Did you find him? Scott! (NORMA *and* CINDY *exchange looks of awe and now* WOODY *enters, the same way, stunned, crosses* L. *and sits on back of sofa.*) Woody? Did you find him? Did you find any sign of him at all? And where's Wally? (*But even as she is asking,* WALLY *enters, with the same stunned attitude.*) Wally!

WALLY. You know! Someone called!

NORMA. How could they? (*Holding up torn telephone wire.*)

WALLY. That's right! Then you don't know. (*Takes* NORMA *by the hand, seats her in chair* L. *concurrent with following dialogue.*)

NORMA. Wally, what happened to your father? (*On verge of tears.*)

WALLY. Mother, you have to prepare yourself. (WALLY *sits on Upstage arm of sofa.*)

NORMA. Where is he? In the hospital? Dead? Tell me!

WALLY. He's in jail!

NORMA. Jail? First, you. Now, your father! We've surpassed the national average, for sure!

WOODY. (*From his daze.*) Haven't you been watching television? NBC and CBS have mobile units on the scene. Chet Huntley said the nation hasn't followed any American this closely since General Patton raced across France.

SCOTT. Of course, in Patton's case we were winning.

NORMA. They're following Walter?

WALLY. You didn't see him burn his checkbook on the steps of the White Plains bank?

WOODY. Or when he let the air out of the tires of every sports car in the parking lot at Saks Westchester?

WALLY. Then he raced to City Hall. And there—there he tried to handcuff himself to the Mayor! That's when they took him off to jail!

NORMA. (*She rises, crosses* C.) Poor Walter—his mind is just blown, blown! (*Decisively; turns to* WALLY.) Wally, you go right down there! Get him out of jail and bring him home!

WALLY. (*Rises from sofa.*) I tried. But there's the matter of bail!

NORMA. WEATHERVANE can certainly go bail for him. The stockholders don't want their president in jail, do they? (WALLY *doesn't answer.*) They do? Clarence Cahill! (WALLY *nods.* NORMA *crosses to* WALLY.) Well,

I'll just call him and tell him—no, wait! Phi Kappa put up their fraternity house as bail for *you*. Why can't *we*—?

WALLY. Uncle Harry wanted to put up *his* house.

NORMA. Isn't that sweet, and after all the things your father's said about him.

WALLY. But it's in Aunt Harriet's name. He's lucky she even signed the proxy.

NORMA. Proxy?

WALLY. Cahill's calling an emergency stockholders meeting for this afternoon. Evidently he's not going to wait for the annual meeting to throw Dad out. And it's all my fault. (WALLY *sits on sofa*.)

NORMA. That vulture! Well, we won't let him—I know! I'll put up *this* house!

WALLY. It may not be necessary. Uncle Harry said there's still one source of money left.

NORMA. (*Sits chair* L.) Who?

WOODY. The union, of course. Where else can you find that much cash these days?

CINDY. But your *dad* said they were threatening to go out on *strike!*

WALLY. They're willing to wait. They'd rather strike against Dad than Clarence Cahill. They like Dad better.

NORMA. When the chips are down, you find out who your real friends are.

WALLY. The union delegate's on his way down now. So Dad may be home at any moment.

(CINDY *sits on table* R.)

NORMA. (*Reassured, she can give vent to some emotion now, crosses down and around to Upstage* R.) To think Chet Huntley compared him to General Patton—

SCOTT. Walter Cronkite kept calling him old Blood-and-Guts Davis.

(NORMA *really gushes tears now*.)

WALLY. Mother, please.
NORMA. (*Tearfully*.) I'm sorry.

SCOTT. Man! Talk about a bad trip!

WOODY. Flipped. Flipped right out!

WALLY. I can't understand it. A mature responsible man his age suddenly going ape. Completely ape!

NORMA. (*Crosses* C.) Wally! That's your *father* you're talking about!

WALLY. Don't I know it! (*He takes his mother by the hand, seats her and then asks:*) Mother—what did we do wrong?

NORMA. (*Standing* C.) I don't know. I just don't know. I've always thought of us as being a well-adjusted homogeneous family unit. (*Beat pause.*) In that McCall's test— "Is Yours A Happy Family?"—we scored ninety-six percent! We were in the "Happy-to-Ecstatic" category. I simply can't understand it . . . I've always tried to give him a feeling of being wanted—included in things —even when he resisted. I just don't understand—unless . . .

WALLY. Yes?

NORMA. (*She crosses to* WALLY *on sofa.*) Wally, I never mentioned this to your father but in that Good Housekeeping test, "Can Your Marriage Last," we—we only scored seventy-four percent.

WALLY. Those tests don't mean anything.

NORMA. (*Turns* R.) Don't they? We were in the "Watch Out For Trouble In Middle Age" category. And here it is, middle age. Somehow, somewhere, I've failed.

CINDY. Mrs. Davis, please, don't blame yourself.

NORMA. These things don't just happen. There has to be a reason. (NORMA *is* U. C.)

WALLY. Well—it—it could be my fault.

NORMA. Wally?

WALLY. (*He rises, crosses* C. *to* NORMA.) Maybe I should have been more of a pal to him. And then there was that time he got all set to give me a sex talk—you know, father-to-son, man-to-man, and I said, You know, you remind me of that character, Jim, on "That's Our Dad."

NORMA. Oh, Wally, you didn't. You know how your father feels about that program.

WALLY. I feel sure now that if I'd let him make a fool of himself he'd have felt better.

SCOTT. My mother tried to tell me. What a fiasco!

WOODY. All my mother kept telling me was, "Don't go near white girls, they'll rape you!"

(CINDY *rises, crosses* L. *to* NORMA.)

CINDY. We handled it differently in my family.

NORMA. We know!

CINDY. We used to discuss it together.

NORMA. Sitting around naked.

CINDY. By that time we wore clothes. Mother always said that was the cause of the divorce . . .

(WALLY *crosses to chair* L., *sits.* WOODY *sits on sofa.*)

NORMA. Divorce—your mother and father?

CINDY. It was a mess. Mother claiming Daddy was impotent. And Daddy claiming it was all due to Mother's nudity kick. (NORMA, *a bit horrified, turns to* WALLY, *who tries to mollify her by gesture.* CINDY, *unaware, goes right on.*) The judge said if they were any more progressive it would have wound up in a double murder. He finally awarded me to my aunt.

NORMA. No!

CINDY. He said my parents were too educated to bring up a child.

NORMA. (*Moving to embrace her.*) Well, don't worry about it. You'll find a good home, right here. We're a nice family—most of the time. (*She looks defensively at* WALLY, *then back to* CINDY. CINDY *nods. They both cross Downstage.*) Do you ever see your parents anymore?

CINDY. Uh-huh.

NORMA. That's nice. You think there's any chance for a reconciliation?

CINDY. I doubt it. Dad remarried.

NORMA. (*Nodding.*) Typical. That article on divorce in McCalls, it said, they remarry on the rebound. I'll bet he's miserable.

CINDY. I don't think so. They have six children.

NORMA. Six children? But you said he was impotent!

CINDY. I never said that. My mother did.

NORMA. True. Well, then there's still hope for Wally.

WALLY. What did you say? Mother! *What did you say?*

NORMA. It's nothing, dear. Just woman talk.

SCOTT. That'll do it. Two women "just talking" can make all the men in the world a minority.

WALLY. Mother! I insist on getting to the bottom of this. That's the second time you've made a reference to *my private life!*

SCOTT. (*Jumps up out of chair* R. *Interrupting, on a thought-plane from another world.*) Wait a minute! *Wait one minute!*

(ALL *turn to him.*)

WALLY. Scott?

SCOTT. It just hit me! In a flash! Like a psychedelic experience!

WOODY. What?

(SCOTT *turns and stares at* NORMA. ALL *turn and stare at her and she suddenly feels that she might be naked.*)

NORMA. Wally? What did I do?

WALLY. There are certain things Scott won't talk about in the presence of *anyone* over thirty.

(ALL *stare at her, till she turns and leaves the room, just stopping to take one last look back to say:*)

NORMA. Nobody *wants* to be over thirty.

(*She exits* U. R. *Once she is gone,* WALLY, CINDY, WOODY *turn to* SCOTT.)

SCOTT. (*Sits on pouf* R.) Shrewd. Clever. Very clever. And he almost got away with it. (WALLY, CINDY, WOODY *react puzzled.*) Your Dad!
  WALLY. Almost got away with what?

(CINDY *and* WOODY *approach* SCOTT.)

SCOTT. Here you are sitting around worrying, "What did we do wrong?" "How did I cause him to flip?" How do we know he did flip? (SCOTT *rises, crosses* C.)
  WALLY. No mature man in his right mind would go out looking like that. Unless—hey—
  SCOTT. Yeah?

(WOODY *and* CINDY *sit on pouf.*)

WALLY. You think *he* was putting *us* on? Blowing *our* minds?
  SCOTT. (*The expert nods, crosses to sofa and sits on sofa back, feet on cushions.*) We had this poly sci professor up at Michigan. Hated the way we dressed. So he began coming to class completely enveloped in a black sack. Never showed his face for two whole weeks. All we heard was his voice. It was eerie. Well, we had to do something. So I worked out a strategy. We *all* started showing up enveloped in sacks. He couldn't take it. Had a nervous breakdown.
  WOODY. What's that got to do with his dad?
  SCOTT. We have to decide on a strategy to deal with him. And if they're getting him out of jail right now we have no time to lose. Now, first, you've got to be firm.
  WALLY. Naturally.
  SCOTT. Now, let's go at this scientifically. Parents are like wild animals. Show the slightest insecurity and they sense it immediately. The first thing he's going to do is threaten.

CINDY. I don't think so. We had a case like that in psych class—

SCOTT. (*He slides down into sofa.*) Cindy! I am an expert on the care and feeding of parents. I have made a study of the species ever since I was eight years old. *I* say he's going to start off by threatening. But we don't budge. Then he'll revert to the usual cliches. "I gave you all the things I never had." "Kids these days have no appreciation." "What we need is another depression." (SCOTT *takes* C. *Stage.*) And only when he runs out of those will he start pleading. And that's when it's going to get dangerous. When they yell and scream, you can tune them out. But when they plead and whine—man!

WOODY. (*On pouf.*) Look, he probably feels like a damn fool and he'll be very happy if we just leave him alone.

CINDY. (*On pouf too.*) The poor man'll be in a post-manic-depression. He'll sneak into the house, slip up to his room, and hide. And I won't blame him.

SCOTT. (*Crosses to them.*) There, you see. He hasn't even shown up yet and you're feeling sorry for him. You've got to be firm!

WOODY. (*Rises.*) Firm. But not cruel.

SCOTT. Did I say cruel? You can shake them up worse with a few kind words. Like the time my Dad and I had been having this running battle, just because I smashed up my sports car. I came home at mid-semester and he was all set for a big fight. Instead, I smiled my biggest smile and said, "Hi, Dad. Great to see you again." *Un*nerved him completely. He didn't know what to expect. Sat there all week-end hiding behind his Wall Street Journal, afraid to come out. Twice I caught him staring at me over the top of it. How relieved he was when I went back to school.

WOODY. I can believe it.

SCOTT. (*Looks askance at* WOODY.) Know your enemy. Right now we've got to face him. Got to tell him we're wise to his strategy and that he failed.

CINDY. We are not going back.

WOODY. And we are not going to apologize.

SCOTT. And we are not going to beg anyone to re-admit us to that school. Now, we've got to make that clear to him! (*Confidentially, to* WALLY.) Remember one thing. We hold the trump card. Our kind of father would rather die than admit his son isn't going to college. And that, my friend, is the big secret.

WOODY. Man, you really do have it figured out.

SCOTT. What Pavlov did with dogs, *I* have done with parents.

WALLY. (*Rises to* SCOTT.) Now, hold on. Just a minute!

SCOTT. (*Fearing* WALLY *is chickening out.*) Wally?

WALLY. He's my father. And my responsibility. I'll handle him.

SCOTT. You're going to need all the help you can get.

(*But they are interrupted by* WALTER's *voice at the front door,* U. L.)

WALTER. (*Offstage.*) You're worse than the Kampus Kops. I didn't need a police escort. (*Coming on, but calling off.*) I could have walked!

(NORMA *rushes on* R. *in response to his lines above.*)

NORMA. Walter, sweetheart——

WALTER. Look what they did to my instrument! (*He holds up the uke which is in two parts, held together only by the strings.* NORMA *puts her arm around him to lead him into the room.*)

NORMA. Walter, what happened? What did they do to you?

WALTER. (*Crosses* D. C.) I kept saying, "I won't talk without a lawyer. I know my rights. You lay a hand on me, that confession won't be worth the paper it's written on!"

NORMA. And what did *they* say?

WALTER. Nothing. Except this one old detective. He said, "Mister, will you please shut up? We're trying to finish this hand."

NORMA. Did they use police brutality, try to intimidate you, or beat you?

WALTER. Mostly, I got the impression they wanted to get rid of me.

WALLY. (*Taking over, on cue from* SCOTT *and* CINDY.) Walter Davis, Senior! This is Walter Davis, Junior, talking. Long Distance. From another generation. (WALTER *turns to* NORMA, *then to* WALLY *with a "What the hell is this?" look on his face.*) Now, you better sit down. Because I've got something to say!

(WOODY *and* SCOTT *close in to* C.)

WALTER. I wish I could, son. But I've got plans and I've got to— (*He starts to exit.*)

WALLY. (*Interrupting.*) First, you'll listen to me! Okay, Dad, so you went out and made a great grandstand play. Just what do you think you've accomplished? I'll tell you. Fell flat on your face, that's what! Made a fool of yourself, that's what! Held yourself up to public ridicule and didn't accomplish one damn thing. You haven't changed our minds. We are not going back. We are not going to apologize!

WALTER. Okay!

WALLY. Okay? What the hell do you mean okay? You're not going to threaten, or argue, plead or whine?

WALTER. (*Starts Upstage.*) I'd like to discuss it with you, son, but I don't have time. I've got to go pack.

WALLY. Pack?

WALTER. (*Stops.*) I've got another pair of these down in the dryer.

WALLY. *Now*, where do you think you're going dressed like that?

WALTER. Why, where it's at, man.

WALLY. Where it's at, man?

WALTER. Up at college, man.

WALLY. College? *My* college?

WALTER. That's it, man! (*He exits.* WALLY *rushes after him to landing.*)

WALLY. Dad! Dad, you can't go up there! Do you hear me? *Mother?*

NORMA. This is more serious than you think. *I'll* talk to him.

(*She exits* U. R. SCOTT *sits on sofa.* WALLY *crosses to him.*)

WALLY. (*Turning on* SCOTT.) Some strategy! Who was your last satisfied client, Nasser?

WOODY. Why would he want to go up there?

WALLY. Man, I can't figure him anymore!

(SCOTT *rises, crosses* R.)

SCOTT. Cool it, group! Cool it. He's bluffing. I know that tactic. *My* father always crawls out on the ledge of the living room window and threatens to jump. Never does.

WALLY. My Dad doesn't bluff.

SCOTT. Don't chicken out now. Stand firm and I guarantee you'll have him pleading with you to go back to another school. Any school.

CINDY. (*Crosses to* WALLY, *with some hesitancy.*) Wally, I want you to know one thing. No matter what happens between your father and you, I won't let it affect our relationship.

(SCOTT *and* WOODY *turn away in disdain.* WOODY *in chair* L.; SCOTT *reclines on sofa.*)

WALLY. Now, what was that? One of those subtle feminine threats? *Your* way of trying to make me conform?

CINDY. Oh, no!

WALLY. You won't dominate me like my mother dominates my dad! (*Moves to pouf. She follows.*)

CINDY. All I meant was—if it would make you feel freer, less middle-class-establishment—if we were *disengaged*—okay.

WALLY. (*Sits on pouf.*) I didn't say that, did I?

CINDY. I know what a sacrifice it was. But I needed some—reassurance.

WALLY. I understand. With your background.

CINDY. (*Nods. Sits on pouf beside him.*) Sometimes I think I'm a psych major not to study other people but myself. And then when I see all the other girls—

WALLY. (*Interrupting.*) All the other girls! I am not going to be a conformist! About love. Or anything else.

CINDY. I'm sorry I spoke to your mother about it.

WALLY. It isn't that. You—you won't think I've wigged out completely, will you?

CINDY. Uh-uh.

WALLY. Okay . . . I won't make love to you because I love you. These days the only way to be a non-comformist in love is *not* to make love. I don't want to wear you like a protest button or a picket sign. What does that make me—a throwback to the Middle Ages?

CINDY. I . . . I think I'm going to cry.

WALLY. Don't. You'll lose your eyelashes.

NORMA. (*Entering.*) Wally! Do something! Now he *has* flipped. Completely flipped!!

(WALLY *and* CINDY *rise.* WALTER *is right behind her, carrying a small suitcase, and in the other hand a bulging laundry bag. He puts suitcase on pouf, laundry on floor and industriously proceeds to take dirty clothes from the laundry bag, select and pack them in the suitcase.*)

WALLY. Dad . . . Dad! Just what do you think you're doing?

WALTER. Packing. I may be there till end of semester. (*Stuffs a dirty shirt into the suitcase.*)

WALLY. But that's the dirty laundry!

WALTER. I ran out of Magi-dirt.

WALLY. Just what do you think you're going to accomplish up there?

WALTER. Stand at the foot of founder's statue and protest. And I don't want to look eccentric. (*Shoves another item into suitcase. Pulling banana out of back pocket.*) Smoke, anyone?

WALLY. Now, Dad, you better listen to me. For your own good. Just what are you going to protest against?

WALTER. Tyranny. Exploitation. Regimentation. I'm for free speech!

SCOTT. Man, *you* are going to picket the Kampus Kops?

WALTER. Man, I am going to picket the Kampus Klowns.

SCOTT. Now you've *got* to stop him!

WALTER. *I'm* striking a blow for freedom. And *against* the tyranny of children. *I* am going to organize, Fathers Incorporated! (*Turning on* WOODY.) And your father is going to be the second member.

WOODY. (*Turning away in anguish.*) Oyyyy!

WALTER. And our slogan is going to be, "Fathers of the World Unite!"

WALLY. Now, Dad, you better cut this out and listen to what I have to say. Or else, I'll—I'll—

WALTER. (*Forcing* GROUP U. L. *against sofa.*) You'll what? Lie on the floor, kick your feet, cry, sulk, hold your breath till you're blue? Well, you are not, no longer, never again, going to intimidate me. (*He shoves* WALLY *into chair* L. *on this last, takes out banana to use as pistol.*) Bang!

SCOTT. (*Figuring* WALTER'S *cracked.*) Oh, he needs help.

WALTER. And I am going to get help. From all the fathers of America. From the cellars and the dens where they are now cowering in fear of their own families—from the used-car lots and the shopping centers—they will rally. As I ride up and down the land— (*He imitates Paul Revere on horseback.*) sounding the alarm, "The Children Are Coming!" And around me, they will fall in. With their golf clubs, their bowling balls, their car keys and any other weapon they happen to have handy. And we will march up Bunker Hill. And there we will dig in and await the attack. From the younger generation. And the order will go down the line. Don't shoot till you see the contempt in their eyes. How superior they feel when they do something heroic, above and beyond the call of duty. Like bring in the morning paper. All the way from the front door. Or back their sports car out of the driveway. So you can pull out and go to work. Or any of the other noble sacrifices that bring the American family close together in times of great emergency. (*Taking his suitcase.*) The only emergency you've ever had in your lifetime, my dear son, was the time I sprained my wrist and couldn't sign checks. Hail and farewell! (*He exits, U. L.*)

WALLY. Dad!

(WALLY, WOODY *and* SCOTT *rush out after* WALTER.)

CINDY. (*Crosses* R. *to* NORMA.) I never thought he'd actually do it.

(NORMA *drops into chair* R. CINDY *stands to her* L.)

NORMA. We'll have to move! To one of those developments for senior citizens. Any place where no one will know us.

(WALLY, WOODY *and* SCOTT *return, carrying* WALTER, *who still carries his suitcase. They set him down firmly.* WOODY *takes away his suitcase.*)

WALLY. You were going? You were actually going up there!

WALTER. Were? *Am*, son, *am* going up there!

WALLY. I won't let you!

WALTER. What about freedom of protest?

WALLY. You can protest right here!

WALTER. (*He crosses* D. C.) What good is a protest unless there's a thousand students, a cowering faculty, TV cameras, Kampus Kops and paddy wagons?

WALLY. Mother, we can't let him leave this house!

NORMA. Not till we move.

WALLY. I am not going to let you go up there and make a fool of yourself!

WALTER. (*Crosses* R. C.) I have as much right to be a fool as you do!

WALLY. You are not going to embarrass this family!

WALTER. I don't think that's a very liberal outlook.

WALLY. No matter what you think, you are not leaving here looking like that!

WALTER. You do.

WALLY. That's different. All the guys do.

WALTER. (*Crosses* L. *to* C.) I just want to be one of the guys, that's all.

SCOTT. Men your age don't go round dressed like that!

WALTER. Why not, if they want to?

WALLY. Because *I* won't let you! Nobody else's father goes around dressed like that. And I am not going to be the laughing stock of the whole campus!!

(GROUP *is lined up* L.)

WALTER. Oh, Norma! Norma, did you hear that? We have failed. We worked and planned to give this precious son of ours all the advantages we never had, all the freedom. And he turns out to be the most dyed-in-the-wool conformist of all.

WALLY. (*No word could hurt worse.*) I am not a conformist!

WALTER. What do you call that? (*Pointing to them all.*) You look like a matched set! Must you be sloppy and dirty, all of you? Couldn't just one of you be neat and dirty? Or sloppy and clean? And now it's not enough that you conform, you want me to conform to your idea of what a father should be. Well, I'll add that to my list of protests!

(*He takes his suitcase to start, but* SCOTT *and* WOODY *take up positions at the door to bar his way.* WALLY *stands in front of them facing his* FATHER.)

WALLY. Dad, if you try to leave this house looking like that, I'll, I'll—

WALTER. You'll what? Refuse to take your allowance? Now, out of my way, all of you! Before *I* give vent to a little hostility— .

(*But* CAHILL *enters* L., *followed by* CHARLOTTE.)

CAHILL. Walter! Thank God, you're still here!!

(WALTER *rushes for window* L. *to escape.*)

WALLY. Mr. Cahill! Do something! Stop him! He wants to go up to my college!

(WALLY *sits on table* R., NORMA *on chair* R.; WOODY, SCOTT, CINDY U. R. *near arch.*)

CAHILL. You can't! Not after what's happened! Walter, do you realize how much your protest has increased television viewing in the east?

WALTER. No. What do you mean? (WALTER *starts moving about the room to elude* CAHILL, *but* CAHILL *follows.*)

CAHILL. The networks had four mobile units following you every step of the way. They took a hot Neilsen. Since he left the house viewing is up sixty-two percent. The demand for antennas has skyrocketed! This afternoon

Sears Roebuck phoned in a big order. It was a master stroke.

(WALTER *crosses* D. C., CAHILL *after him.*)

WALTER. I was only trying in some small way to let parents know—

CAHILL. And you did! Why, when we were holding that emergency stockholders' meeting—

WALTER. Your dissident stockholders' group?

CAHILL. When they watched you on TV—*doing* all the things, *saying* all the things they wanted to say all these years but were afraid to—did you know that ninety-six percent of our stockholders have teen-age children?

WALTER. No. I didn't know they were that active!

CAHILL. So you spoke up for us too. And when you increased our sales besides—now, they're afraid you'll leave the company—

WALTER. (*Starts to go.*) Exactly what I intend to do.

CAHILL. (*Comes to him.*) Walter, you can't leave the company! The stockholders won't stand for it! *I* won't stand for it!

CHARLOTTE. (*Reprovingly.*) Clar-ence—

CAHILL. (*When MRS. VULTURE talks, he listens.*) What I mean is—won't you please stay? Walter? For the good of the company? For the good of White Plains?

CHARLOTTE. Clarence, tell it like it is.

CAHILL. All right, Charlotte. Walter—you know our three sons. All over twenty-five. All married. All still in graduate school!

CHARLOTTE. They're very education-oriented.

CAHILL. Let's put it this way. They're definitely not *job*-oriented! For the last six years, I have been trying to get up the courage to tell them what you showed the world in a few magnificent hours.

CHARLOTTE. Did you know Walter Cronkite called you Old-Blood-and-Guts Davis?

WALTER. No, Charlotte, darling. I'll demand equal time and call him a few things.

CAHILL And, Walter, another thing. Telephones are ringing all over White Plains. People are talking. There've been meetings. You can have the nomination for mayor on either ticket. Or both!

CHARLOTTE. (*To* NORMA.) His confrontation with the younger generation has inspired us all!

CAHILL. Think what it would mean to Weathervane to have such a man as president. We could change our slogan. "Weathervane, the Company That Cares . . . for Parents!" Walter, you *have* to do it. (*Beat pause.*) Walter?

WALTER. (*He crosses down behind sofa to* D. L.) I don't know. I have miles to go before I sleep.

WALLY. (*Crosses* D. L. C.) Dad, you just can't go up to college!

WALTER. (*Crosses to him.*) But I've got a whole new career waiting for me.

WALLY. You'll ruin my *college* career!

(SCOTT *withdraws to a corner by himself, not joining in the plea.*)

CINDY. None of us will dare to show our faces on any campus in this country again!

WOODY. (*Rises, crosses* C.) You promised my father you'd get us back into school!

WALLY. Please, Dad? Don't go?

WALTER. I'm just getting the hang of it. I like it. Is my hair on straight?

WALLY. Dad? Please?

NORMA. Walter, your son is pleading with you.

CINDY. (*Crosses* D. C.) Please, Mr. Davis, for Wally's sake?

WOODY. For all our sakes!

WALTER. Well—I don't want to be unreasonable. I'm willing to negotiate.

GROUP. Anything!

WALLY. Anything within reason!

WALTER. (*Taking off his wig, puts it on coffee table* L.) Okay, let's get to the bargaining table. And, Norma, *you* have to agree to the terms, too.

NORMA. Yes, Walter.

(GROUP *adjusts* R.)

WALTER. (*Crosses* C.) From now on, things are going to be different around here. In the first place, this is no longer a "homogeneous family unit." Or any of those other big words! (*Covering both* NORMA *and* CHARLOTTE *with his glance.* SCOTT *is* U. R.) No more "father figure." Or "mother figure." Just father, mother, and son. And we don't "communicate" or have "dialogues." We just talk.

NORMA. Yes, Walter.

WALTER. (*To* WALLY.) From now on, if we have something to say, we *say* it. We don't *sing* it!

CINDY. Yes, sir!

WALTER. And not everybody with a guitar is automatically qualified to be Secretary of State.

WALLY. Okay, Dad!

WALTER. And nobody is going to use the word "materialistic" or "money-oriented" around here, unless he is willing to give up his sports car, work his way through school and close out all charge accounts.

CAHILL. Oh, I wish my sons could hear that! All three of them!

WALTER. (*Turning his attention to* NORMA *now.*) And there's another word we're not going to use around here. Castrated. (CHARLOTTE *gasps, hides her face in* CLARENCE'S *chest.*) I don't like it. I don't like the way it sounds. I don't like what it stands for. I don't think it'll do me any good. *Did you hear that, Norma?*

NORMA. Yes, dear.

WALTER. Now, I have already arranged for the four of you to be readmitted to school, provided you go back and apologize to Dean Stallings.

WALLY. We will not give up our freedom of protest.

CINDY. Right!

WALTER. I never asked you to. Did I?

WALLY. That's true.

WALTER. Just exercise it in a way that lets other people have their freedom too. And apologize to all deans who wind up in traction.

WALLY. But Dad—!

(CINDY and WOODY *support him with ad-libs of dissent.*)

WALTER. Okay, the deal is off. I don't consider it negotiating unless I win every point. (*He moves to get his bag and wig from coffee table* L.)

WALLY. Okay, Dad! You win. We'll apologize.

WALTER. (*Meets* WALLY *at* C.) Son, there was one thing you said that really hurt. About running out. Getting so wrapped up chasing the buck that I bought my way out with my own son. I hated it when you said it—because it was true. And I'm sorry. I won't let it happen again. (*He holds out hand. They shake.*) I'm cutting your allowance tomorrow.

(*They laugh, then embrace.*)

WALLY. Okay, Group, we're going back!

(CINDY, WOODY *move to get their things but* SCOTT *has his gear already and comes forward,* D. R. *and around to* WALTER, *at* C.)

SCOTT. Not me, man! I never go back.

WALLY. Scott!

SCOTT. (*Moving to* WALTER.) One father like you can louse it up for everyone! I'm cutting out. I think I'll try a foreign college. Paris, maybe. The Sorbonne.

WALTER. Good! Now DeGaulle will have a *reason* for hating us.

(SCOTT *exits.*)

WOODY. (*Approaching to shake hands with* WALTER.) Thanks for everything, Mr. Davis.

WALTER. Now, Woody, you stay off your feet as much as you can, you hear?

(WOODY *starts to exit, reacts to what* WALTER *said, then exits.* CINDY *approaches* WALTER.)

CINDY. I'm sorry for all the trouble, Mr. Davis. And thanks. For Wally's sake. And mine too. (*She kisses him on the cheek.*)

WALTER. Did he say engaged? (*She nods.*) Good! (*He kisses her on the lips.*) Man, that really is a girl!

(CINDY *moves* L. *to* NORMA.)

NORMA. (*Confidentially.*) Try wearing skirts, dear.

CINDY. Minis?

NORMA. The minier the better.

WALLY. Mother! (*He gestures impatiently to* CINDY, *who joins him, and they exit together.*)

CAHILL. (*Crossing to* WALTER.) Now, Walter, the stockholders have to have an answer.

WALTER. Tell them they'll have a new model, a new slogan and the same old president.

CAHILL. Good! Good! They'll be delighted! The union'll be happy too. They wouldn't feel right striking against anyone else!

(*He starts to join* CHARLOTTE *at the door. And only after he's moved does* WALTER *react to his line with a resentful take.*)

CHARLOTTE. (*Crosses to* NORMA.) Norma, darling . . .

NORMA. Yes, Charlotte, darling . . .

CHARLOTTE. The girls were hoping that you'd be willing to make your speech now under a new title, "Eyeball to Eyeball, Confrontation with the Younger Generation."

CAHILL. (*Tapping her on shoulder.*) Charlotte, unless you can say it in words of one syllable, why don't you shut up? (*Surprised at his own forthrightness, he says to* WALTER.) I've been wanting to say that since the day we got married.

CHARLOTTE. (*Starts to say:*) Speechwise I'm absolutely speechless--- (*But* CLARENCE *takes her hand and drags her off.*)

(*Left alone,* NORMA *and* WALTER *turn to look at each other.*)

NORMA. Oh, Walter, I've been terrible to you all these years, haven't I?

WALTER. You haven't been any worse than any other American woman is to her husband.

NORMA. Is there anything I can do to make up for it?

WALTER. Well, we could sit in front of the fireplace every evening. And burn a few magazines. Without reading them.

NORMA. Whatever you say, dear. (*She kisses him. He embraces her, returns the kiss. During the embrace,* NORMA *suddenly straightens.*) Good heavens! Is today Wednesday?

WALTER. I think so. Why?

NORMA. Why? Wednesday! The opera! Lincoln Center! Hurry! Put on your dinner jacket, we'll be late! (NORMA *starts for the stairs to go up and get dressed.* WALTER *does not move. She stops, turns.*) Walter?

WALTER. The opera. Lincoln Center. I'll have to look my best for that. (*He picks up his black wig and starts preening it with his hand. She gets the message.*) I'll get this washed and set.

NORMA. On the other hand, sweetheart—

WALTER. Yes, sweetheart? (*He combs. She comes down to him.*)

NORMA. Maybe we better stay home.

WALTER. That's a good idea.

NORMA. (*Reaching for wig.*) I'll fix us a nice simple dinner, sweetheart.

WALTER. (*Slapping her hand away, gently.*) That'll be nice, dear.

NORMA. And you can just sit and relax, dear.

WALTER. I'll do that, sweetheart.

NORMA. (*She starts out.*) I'll call you when dinner's ready, sweetheart.

WALTER. Thank you, dear. (*She exits. He holds the wig, studies it a moment, then:*) Who says blondes have more fun?

*CURTAIN COMES DOWN*
*QUICKLY FOR END OF PLAY*

## PROP LIST

3 guitars—(2 gut string, 1 steel)
2 standard ukes (1 breakaway)
2 knapsacks (dunnage stuffed)
1 pair prop sneakers
1 suitcase (Walter)
1 antenna (pre-fab with base)
1 weathervane and cock (to top above antenna)
2 "Reader's Digest" magazines
4 prop-headline newspapers
6 pairs sunglasses
14 display 12-oz. beer cans
3 empty pizza cartons
1 muslin laundry bag (with dunnage)
1 12-in. tambourine
1 set small bongo drums
4 protest signs—

> THERE ARE NO DIRTY WORDS,
> ONLY DIRTY MINDS
> LSD—BETTER LIVING THROUGH
> CHEMISTRY
> BACK UP YOUR RIGHT TO SHACK UP
> POT? WHY NOT?

1 protest sign—FREE SPEECH FOR PARENTS
1 sandwich-board protest sign—

*Front side reads:*

> BACK UP YOUR LOVE WITH
> THE BACK OF YOUR HAND

*Opposite side:*

> DOCTOR SPOCK IS A CROCK

Door chimes
Telephone ring effect
Plastic banana

## ONSTAGE PROPS

9-ft. sofa
6 throw pillows
Twin marble-top coffee tables
Woven armchair
Telephone table and dial telephone (phone rips out)
Padded armchair and reinforced pouf
Twin end tables
Large Roman end table
Twin 6-ft. display cases
Antique hall mirror, seat and rack comb
4 framed flower pictures on staircase
4 framed circular tiles by library
1 set (36) Britannica "Great Books"
1 wrought-iron chandelier
Pair wrought-iron sconces
4 umbrellas
2 tennis ashtrays
1 silver cigarette box
1 silver lighter
Bulk used books and magazines
21 articles of "Danish modern," "cottage" and "Boutique" type
   pottery
3 articles Mexican pottery
1 Peruvian pottery (bull)
1 India-Pakistan jewel box
1 woven jewel box
1 fur deer
1 fur bull
Drapery
Floral arrangement in bowl to hang in alcove
1 book—Dr. Spock

# COSTUME PLOT

## NORMA:

*Act One—Scene One*
Emerald-green street dress
Brown leather slippers
Pearl necklace, earrings (gold and turquoise)
Dark-rimmed glass frames
White handkerchief—nylon hosiery

*Act One—Scene Two*
Turquoise negligee nightgown
Turquoise bedroom slippers and handkerchief
Nylon hosiery

*Act Two*
Two-piece street suit trimmed with turquoise binding
Turquoise and rhinestone small broach
Brown leather slippers (same as in Act One)
Pearl necklace and earrings (same as in Act One)
Nylon hosiery

## WALTER:

*Act One—Scene One*
Business suit
Jacket-trousers
Blue shirt
Cap
Black oxfords

*Act One—Scene Two*
Maroon silk bathrobe
House slippers

*Act Two*
Hippy attire
Blue dungarees
Grey sweatshirt
Cutaway coat
Several strings of beads
White sneakers
Black wig

CINDY:

*Act One*
Light-blue pants
Blue jacket
Brown cap
Sweater
Brown leather slippers
Shirt with lettering

*Act Two*
Blue pants
Peach sweater
Beads
Flower in hair
Brown leather slippers (same as Act One)

CHARLOTTE:

*Act One*
Peach-colored two-piece suit (street dress)
White gloves
Multicolored hat
Handbag
Brown slippers
Rhinestone pin

*Act Two*
Grey jersey street dress
Silver slippers
Long gold chain
Rhinestone and jade broach and earrings (to match)
Small handbag

CLARENCE:

*Act One and Act Two*
Blue business suit
White shirt
Tie
Black shoes
Sox

COSTUME PLOT

WOODY:

*Act One*
Blue dungarees
Jacket
Printed shirt
Suede shoes
Hat

*Act Two—Scene One*
Blue dungarees
Print shirt

*Act Two—Scene Two*
Same as Act One

WALLY:

*Act One—Scene One*
Tan pants
Sweat shirt
Tan corduroy jacket
White and red socks
Suede shoes
Hat

*Act One—Scene Two*
Printed pajamas
Robe

*Act Two*
Red knit shirt
Plus same as Act One

SCOTT:

*Act One—Scene One*
Brown jacket
Brown corduroy pants
Brown leather boots
Blue work shirt
Hat

*Act Two—Scene One*
Printed pajamas

*Act Two—Scene Two*
Same as Act One

No one shall make any changes in this title(s) for the purpose of production. No part of this book may be reproduced, stored in a retrieval system, scanned, uploaded, or transmitted in any form, by any means, now known or yet to be invented, including mechanical, electronic, digital, photocopying, recording, videotaping, or otherwise, without the prior written permission of the publisher. No one shall share this title(s), or any part of this title(s), through any social media or file hosting websites.

For all inquiries regarding motion picture, television, online/digital and other media rights, please contact Concord Theatricals Corp.

## MUSIC AND THIRD-PARTY MATERIALS USE NOTE

Licensees are solely responsible for obtaining formal written permission from copyright owners to use copyrighted music and/or other copyrighted third-party materials (e.g., artworks, logos) in the performance of this play and are strongly cautioned to do so. If no such permission is obtained by the licensee, then the licensee must use only original music and materials that the licensee owns and controls. Licensees are solely responsible and liable for clearances of all third-party copyrighted materials, including without limitation music, and shall indemnify the copyright owners of the play(s) and their licensing agent, Concord Theatricals Corp., against any costs, expenses, losses and liabilities arising from the use of such copyrighted third-party materials by licensees. For music, please contact the appropriate music licensing authority in your territory for the rights to any incidental music.

## IMPORTANT BILLING AND CREDIT REQUIREMENTS

If you have obtained performance rights to this title, please refer to your licensing agreement for important billing and credit requirements.